# ZEPH

# ZEPH

A. L. Barker

HUTCHINSON
London

This edition first published in 1992 by
Hutchinson

**Random House UK Limited**
20 Vauxhall Bridge Road, London SW1V 2SA

**Random House Australia (Pty) Ltd**
20 Alfred Street, Milsons Point, Sydney, NSW 2061, Australia

**Random House New Zealand Ltd**
18 Poland Road, Glenfield, Auckland, New Zealand

**Random House South Africa (Pty) Ltd**
PO Box 337, Bervlei, 2012, South Africa

A CIP catalogue record for this book is available from the British Library.

ISBN 0 09 174642 6

Set in Plantin by Pure Tech Corporation, Pondicherry, India
Printed and bound in Great Britain by
Biddles Ltd, Guildford and King's Lynn

If 'in great things even to have wished is enough', this book is for those for whom wishing is not enough.

I'll be classical, I'll be popular, I'll be the unintelligent woman's Iris Murdoch. Not this year, next year or the year after. Sometime. But never never. No one shall stop me. From the gate to the end of the railings, counting each upright, on the present scale it works out at sometime.

It's not exactly a game, it's not exactly anything, it leaves room for doubt and luck and hope. Some people use tea-leaves and animal guts: properly manipulated, a sheep's alimentary canal will answer questions about the future. My method is non-messy. I use pavement blocks – counting them to the kerb or the next manhole cover; car colours – yes if the next one's blue, no if it's red; bald men, white lines, black babies and the bathroom tiles. I use anything and anyone that can be counted.

I was using the method to take my mind off a party I was on my way to. I dread parties. This one had been decreed by my mother.

'You must go. They particularly asked for you.'

'Who asked?'

'People think it weird when you won't join in and have fun with others of your own age.'

'I don't want to join in that kind of fun.'

'Don't be pompous.' A light laugh. 'No man is an island and certainly no woman is. You ought to understand what goes on in the world. I told Natalie Spilsbury you'd go. She'd like you to keep an eye on Kate. The girl's over-eating. It's a phase, she's always into something.'

'Bulimia.'

'What?'

'It's what she's into.'

A deep breath, the echo of a sigh. 'Do go, Zephrine, and try to enjoy yourself. To please me.'

It might mean that she wanted me to enjoy myself or that

1

she wanted me to be groovy. Short of re-birth there's little chance of that.

The young Spilsburys dug their own groove, it throbbed to the beat of the Loved and Envied, Dick Spilsbury's favourite group. The beat could be heard low down, coming from under the hedge seemingly. But as I approached their house the sound grew tall, reaching into the sky, into Concorde's flight-path, where would be the end of it. I felt sorry for the neighbours.

As I opened the garden gate a boy sprang out of the bushes and caught me round the waist crying 'Hosanna!'

I said, 'Are you Jewish?'

He released me, muttering. 'Hell, I thought you were Rosanna from the BBC. She's coming to record my Kitchamajig Concerto.'

I said, 'What?' but he was gone. The front door stood open on Kate Spilsbury sitting on the stairs.

'Hi,' she said, without enthusiasm.

'Is it someone's birthday?'

'Why?'

'What's the party in aid of?'

'Nothing. We felt like one.'

'Who was that I just saw? Said he was expecting to be recorded by the BBC.'

'He plays on spoons and egg-whisks. Gruesome.'

'I'd like to hear him.'

Kate shifted something from one cheek to the other. 'Fetch me some food from Dick's room, will you? I've got to stay here.'

'Why?'

'To watch for gatecrashers.'

'What will you do if they come?'

'Bring them in, of course. I'd like a burger, any old burger, and a cream horn.'

I had to step over a couple at the top of the stairs. Remembering my mother's injunction I took note of what they were doing. They looked unhappy, the girl bent backwards with the edge of the stair cutting across her spine, the boy hooped over her, his heels bursting out of his trainers as he tried to get purchase on the tread below.

'Excuse me.' Certainly understanding is required, my mother was marginally right. With the Loved and Envied to guide me,

I opened a door into a bathroom where a girl was shaving her armpits.

'Party's next door,' she said, not looking up.

I question the word 'party': it can be people uniting for politics or for a game, or a cause, it can be the party of the first part, or party to a crime, or a person unknown and unsexed, or just memorable moments in the lives of the Spilsburys.

Dick's door was plastered with warnings. 'Private, Do Not Disturb', 'Keep Out', 'Sod Off', 'Scram!' For better, for worse – worse, my mother would say, because it sets me apart – I can't subscribe to that kind of gratuitous rudeness, putting up the first shots as if life's a war. I knocked and went in.

The few people in the room didn't fill it, but the Loved and Envied did. They were in every crook, cranny, rumple and crease. Sorting out people from the sound, I saw Dick Spilsbury, wearing pyjamas and a building-site bowler. He flipped his hand at me. Two boys scuffled on the floor. They fought like puppies, biting with soft mouths, butting each other, giggling. A girl sat cross-legged on the bed, smiling to herself. Something smouldered between her fingers and smelled sweet. A man called to me. 'Who might you be?'

'Zeph.'

The man, who was sitting astride a chair, stood up with one uneasy movement and came close. He wore a black jersey and ginger cords balding at the knee. He looked old enough to know better, but were I to say so, he would say better than what and I should have to say better than to use drugs and it was none of my business except virtually. I need the *idea* of what drug-taking's like. In my line of country I need ideas.

'I suppose you haven't any skins?' he said.

'Sorry?'

'We're out of papers. We're waiting for a connection from Crystal Palace.'

Dick Spilsbury, beating time with the Loved and Envied, shouted 'Where's your sister?'

'I haven't got a sister.'

'The one with piano legs.'

'I don't know anyone with piano legs.'

'I saw you with her at Heathrow.'

'That was Nell Peppiatt. She went to America. She has nice legs.'

'Like a piano.'

'Dick's fond of music,' said the man in the black jersey.

'Is there anything to eat?'

'Everything's gone. Are you hungry?'

'It's not for me, it's for Kate.'

'Like a drink?'

I said I would and when he went to get it I asked the privately smiling girl who he was.

'I forget. I forget who *I* am. I forget everything. It's heaven.' She was gazing raptly between the bedposts, as if Nirvana was contained by Dick Spilsbury's bedstead. I wanted to ask which it most resembled, dreaming or dying, but I thought she was unlikely to know enough about dying to make the comparison, and dreaming's easy, there's no need to smoke hash to do it. Anyway, her eyes were wide open, her eyelids didn't quiver, which is said to be the outward indication of a dreamer.

'Here.' He had brought wine in a pottery mug and a china cup. He handed the cup to me.

'That girl says she's forgotten who she is.'

'It's a big step forward.'

'Have you forgotten who you are?'

'Dalton Toplady, that's me.' His face was like a peppered egg, he had a deeply pitted skin, in each pit was a black grain. 'Drink up, that cup leaks and you're losing wine fast.'

'It tastes funny, is it spiked?'

'No, corked.' He laughed a Basil Brush laugh. 'What did you say your name is?'

'Zeph. I'm here for the experience.'

'Aren't we all.'

'My interest is professional. I'm going to drink this.' I felt ennobled as I drained the cup to the dregs which tasted like blood clots.

'Are you doing a survey?'

'I'm going to be a writer.'

'You have to get looped to write?'

'This once.'

'Let me help.' He emptied his wine into my cup. 'It's a brave thing you're doing.'

4

'A writer must be familiar with every side of life.' It's the official view and I knew I had better not find it intimidating.

'What would you like to know about this side?'

I was wondering if hairs grew out of the pits or alongside. 'What happened to your face?'

'Have I got a smut?'

'You've got hundreds of smuts. How did you manage it?'

'None of your business.'

'But it is.' I was becoming aware of a valuable new percipience cutting through to the heart of this matter which was one particular pore in the centre of his chin. He had a chin like a bell-push. 'A writer must be totally receptive.'

'It leaves you wide open.'

'A writer embraces all experience.'

'Tell you what.' He leaned towards me, I could have put a finger on his chin and rung the bell. 'Drink up and I'll give you something to write about.'

The boys fighting on the floor rolled under the bed, the girl sitting on it was still sitting, Dick Spilsbury was shouting football shouts and the pop sound had reached a tempo prior to the bursting of a blood vessel.

'I'll have to sit down.'

'Not here.'

'I like it here.' That was true. I wouldn't have believed I could so swiftly embrace what had so recently been offensive and perverse, it was part of my new percipience. 'I'm changed, my mother would approve.'

'That's important?'

'Relatively.'

'Relative to what?'

'Relative to she's my mother.' I regretted that my new percipience could stretch to that sort of thing.

Toplady shot out both arms and stopped me sitting on the floor. 'It's too noisy here, let's go somewhere else.'

'Don't you recognize the generation beat? Every generation has its own. Ours is low down and primal.'

'You read that in a book.'

'I shall write it in a book.'

'Let's go where we can talk. I know a place.'

I said, 'There's someone in the bathroom.'

He bundled me into the passage, flung open a door and pushed me before him as if I was a sack of something. This room was in darkness save for a huge shape swimming towards us.

I cried, 'There's a denizen of the deep in here!'

Toplady switched on the light and I saw that I was looking at our reflections in a mirror. We were in a bedroom. The king-sized bed was covered with a ruched satin quilt, a pompadour doll reclined on the pillows.

'This is the master bedroom, Spilsbury *mère* and *père* are away for the weekend.'

I weaved over to the dressing-table mirror. 'I saw a hump-backed whale.'

'Lie down and take it easy.'

'I don't just observe, you know, I absorb. I absorb what I need. I needed a hump-backed whale.' I picked up a powder-puff on a stick. 'If I was writing about Mrs Spilsbury I'd absorb this.'

'She'd sue you.'

'She wouldn't recognize herself. The way I write there'd be other people mixed with her, I take the best and the worst from each and make somebody new.'

'Come to bed.'

'With you?'

'Why not?'

I thought, here's this perfect stranger – accepting that ignorance can be perfect – proposing a gross indecency on the marital bed of my mother's best friend. Surely an absorbable experience.

'I promise you', he said earnestly, 'it won't be the same old same old.'

'I'm not sure I can contribute anything.'

He punched the pillows. 'We're wasting time.'

'Is it like dancing? If you don't know the steps, you follow your partner and do as he does?'

'You've left it late finding out.'

'I've thought about it in general terms.'

'Don't worry, I'll fill you in on the details. We'll do whatever you like. What would you like to do?'

'What was in the wine?'

'An Indian love-drug.'

6

The satin quilt was now a sea ruched with little waves. I longed to sink beneath it. I thought is this *desire*? I sank to a sitting posture and he put his arms round me and toppled us both backwards, then sat up to drag the pompadour doll from under his neck. 'The damned thing bit me!'

Manhandled, the doll gave birth to Mrs Spilsbury's pink satin nightdress. The idea of Mrs Spilsbury, a woman with a nose like a tomahawk, desiring among these same pillows, made me go cold. 'I don't think we ought to be here.'

I would have struggled up, but he swung a leg over me as if I was a bicycle and held me down by my wrists. 'Stop worrying!'

'How will I feel afterwards?'

'Great. I've got certificates for it.'

'How will I feel about life? And death?'

'Death?'

'There are these three things everyone must do: get born, make love, and die. If you're not going to make love because of religion or because you've been passed over, it's still the biggest thing you never did. I realize that. The question is, how do you make it?'

'I'll show you. I'm not called Toplady for nothing.' The black specks amalgamated for a kiss.

'You promised me something to write about.' It was obvious to me that there was a deep connection between his face and Mrs Spilsbury's nightdress and I would be required to analyse it, it was the sort of thing I would be doing, tracing the labyrinthine workings of the mind. 'I'd like to write about your face. Tell me how it happened.'

'I put sulphur and potash in the hollow stem of a big key, stuck a nail in the end and swung the key round my head. It hit a wall and exploded and I was sacked from school as a danger to the community. Will that do?'

There was a pause which I prolonged out of respect for his confidence. I had been hoping to warm towards him, but a boy blowing himself up with a key isn't endearing.

'Thank you for telling me. If we're to be lovers, I think I should know something about you.'

The specks came together to line the folds of his grin. 'So now you know, let's be what you said.'

7

'Of course I've read about explicit sex, but I shouldn't myself go into details unless they were vital to my theme. A writer can't avoid love. There are so many kinds, aren't there? Could you just –' Men are heavy, I hadn't ever had one pushing my ribs into my backbone before. 'I can't breathe –'

'Keep still, it's all taken care of.' Under a jell of sweat his face turned as pink as Mrs Spilsbury's nightdress.

'If we *made* love, I mean if we created it, we'd be God. We'd all be God.'

'We are.'

'What do we use? Do we mix it like a cake? Love can mean zero, it means that too in crossword clues. But you can't make nothing, so it can't be all or nothing, it's got to be all *and* nothing.'

He raised himself on his hands, mercifully removing his weight, letting my ribs rejoin my breastbone. When I was able to take a breath, I said, 'It's the fire of the soul. How do we get the fire started?'

I overheard Mavis, my mother – a mavis is a songbird, why did they call her that? – and Mrs Spilsbury, the woman of the nightdress, talking about us, their children. They dissolved our reputations.

'There's an atmosphere after they've had one of their parties.'

'Atmosphere?'

'I'm obliged to open the windows.'

'There's a smell?'

'I don't know how to describe it. A disturbance. The house takes a while to settle down.'

'There's a mess?'

'Certainly not. I made it clear that they're welcome to have their friends on the strict understanding that they leave every-thing as they find it and as we would wish to find it. Only on one occasion did we come home to chips in the bonsai. Denis confiscated their electronics for a fortnight.'

'It makes such a difference having a man's support.'

'I took the decision, Denis removed the apparatus. I'm quite capable of doing what I think best, but it's fitting that he is seen to share the responsibility. These are crucial years for adolescents, a lot depends on the unity of the family.'

'Zephrine is at the awkward stage, uncommunicative and boorish. She suspects me. Her father spoiled her.'

'In what way?'

'In every way. She and I were close when she was small. I remember the moment she began to draw away. We were on the beach, playing a game with pebbles when she rounded on me crying, "You're supposed to let me win!" Her little face was twisted with hate. She'd forgotten about it next minute, but I never have.'

'A childish tantrum.'

'Her father encouraged her to believe she could do anything. She is over-ambitious.'

'In all probability she wants nothing more than to become a wife and mother. It's what girls have always wanted but nowadays they daren't admit it. Kate tells me it's womanism as opposed to feminism.'

'Zephrine has delusions of glory. I tell her it's unhealthy to shut herself in her room for hours on end. She says, what do I mean by health.'

'It is an attempt to discredit the old values for no other reason than that they are old.'

'I don't know what she thinks, I know it's not what I think, and it's not what I can understand her thinking.'

'The important thing is to leave one's children in no doubt about one's own views. They will have to subscribe to them eventually.'

'I can't talk to her. She looks at me as if I'm a stranger.'

'Kate and Richard follow the current trends of folly, one may as well try to turn the tide as try to impose moderation at this stage.'

'Zephrine has never been foolish *enough*.'

On Saturdays I don't have to rush off to work and my mother and I have breakfast together. We had a letter each, mine was from Nell Peppiatt. She writes pages.

'Mine's from Gladys,' said my mother. 'She likes to keep in touch, she thinks we're two of a kind.'

Mavis, my mother, would like to have been wayward, but there wasn't time. She married my father when she was eight-

9

een. She thinks I'm a battleground for their genes, hers bright and shining, his grey and gristly.

'What has Nell to say?'

'She's taken up with a man.'

'Taken up?'

'She's living with him in California. He's a sculptor. Nell's working in a boutique.'

'I wouldn't have given her credit for a serious artistic sense.'

'I expect she's better off without one in a boutique.'

'I was thinking of her attraction for the sculptor.'

'Their minds may not meet, but other parts have. He's made her pregnant.'

'Don't be vulgar.'

'There's nothing vulgar about pregnant. It means full of promise, of thoughts and emotions.'

'I imagine it's part of her life-style. Young people don't believe in waiting. "I want it now" – isn't that the saying?'

'If she wants a baby now, she's got to keep on wanting it tomorrow and tomorrow and tomorrow. Like not having a puppy just for Christmas.'

'It's unprincipled and she's gone too far, but she is living. Tell me about the party.'

'Someone tried to seduce me. He said his name was Toplady. Dick Spilsbury says it's more a matter of what he'd like to do than what he does.' She slit open her letter, there was marmalade on the knife, so I knew she was offended. 'What kind are you and Gladys two of?'

'We are both alone.'

She says things like that to demolish me so that she will be able to remake me and her genes will win.

'When did you last see your father?'

I thought of the picture of the boy in a blue satin suit standing on a stool before Roundhead soldiers. 'You know that he has moved into a house immediately opposite where Gladys lives.'

'No, I didn't. And he couldn't have known.'

'Didn't you stop to think how I would feel, how I do feel, about you going to him? Behind my back?'

I made a business of folding Nell's letter. 'It was nothing to do with you.'

'It is everything to do with me!'

'Your do and mine aren't the same any more. They used to meet at certain points when I was too young to judge for myself.'

'Judge!' She threw the letter across the table. 'You'd better read this.'

Cousin Gladys types her letters and divides them into subject-related paragraphs. The first paragraph went on about old age – hers; the next was about her hip operation and the perfidy of the NHS. The next was business-like.

You may rest assured that the matter you entrusted me with will be treated in the utmost confidence. I shall refer to the person concerned as the Subject. He is living in the house opposite, which is let out into apartments. The tenants are a mixed lot and the Subject is rapidly losing any resemblance of respectability. I am in a position to observe from my bedroom window. I take my knitting to usefully occupy my time. He, or she – his common-law wife or concubine, she is black as coal – neglect to draw the curtains at night. They make no secret. What takes place at the back of the house I can only conjecture and no doubt that is just as well.

Mavis, you would be disgusted. She dresses, if you can call it dressing, in coloured rags and animal skins – from the cats that go missing I shouldn't wonder. I have seen her perform what I believe is called a belly-dance.

I made discreet enquiry of the milkman and was informed that the Subject goes by the name we both know and which' we might have hoped he would have the decency to change in the circumstances. I can only assume he has forgotten that I live in this road, for surely even he would not knowingly expose you to such infamy.

You have my deepest sympathy, the more so because of a fact which I would prefer not to have to apprise you of. But it is my duty to tell you that Zephrine is a visitor to that house.

I said, 'Gladys is an old witch, you don't want to believe everything she says.'

'But you go?'

'Now and then.'

11

'What do you do there?'

'Talk.'

'About me?'

'He said he would expect me to take sides and he would expect me to take yours, so we more or less arranged not to talk about you.'

'The Creature who lives with him, what about her?'

'Maria?'

'She's called Maria?' My mother laughed unpleasantly.

My father calls me Zeph. He always has. Before I learned to read, my mother used to read to me. She didn't do it well, she couldn't put in expression or diversify the characters: Rupert Bear and the Wicked Stepmother both spoke with her voice, and The Girl Who Trod on the Loaf went down into the underworld with no hint of stress. I used to listen with my eyes shut so as not to see her holding the book which she did as though it was alive and grubby.

She would challenge me. 'Are you asleep?'

'Yes.'

'What did the princess say when the prince asked who she was?'

'Zeph.'

'Of course she didn't.'

'She did, she said Zeph!'

'I gave you a beautiful name, is it too much trouble to use it?'

My father was reared in Jamaica where his father owned a bauxite concession. My father was still a boy when the family came back to England, he said he had always been happy in Jamaica, it was almost Paradise he said. But my mother didn't want to hear about the animals and flowers and people.

'What have they got that we haven't? Only the sun. Of course they're kind-hearted, of course they're happy, why wouldn't they be? It's not virtue, it's geography.'

She said his daydreams shut her out. He wanted her to share them and I couldn't see why she couldn't. To me they were a series of pictures, like a comic, like *Beano*. I took them with the same grain of salt. I used to badger him to tell me about when he was little. 'What did you have for breakfast?'

'Coffee and bananas.'

'What was in your garden?'

'A silk-cotton tree.'

'You can't have a silk tree and you can't have a cotton tree.'

'In that country you can.'

'You can only have a wooden tree in any country.'

'In that country there are all kinds of trees. There's even a woman's-tongue tree. They call it that because the leaves are so long.'

It would have been better if they could have quarrelled, but quarrelling takes two and she couldn't get him started. He just waited, as if he was waiting for her to get over hiccups. If they could have quarrelled they could have made up.

I wasn't turning out as she had named me. I've always had a solid figure and by the time I was ten I had a lot on my mind as well. I used to come straight home from school and go to my room and lie on my bed reading. In fine weather she packed me off to play with other children. I'd sneak into the garden shed and sit on the Atco.

'What are you doing?' she said when she found me.

'Writing a story.'

'How nice. What's it about?'

'A man who shuts his wife in the wardrobe.'

'Why?'

'He doesn't like her.'

'And then?'

'She comes out with different clothes on.'

'She'd have a choice, wouldn't she – being in the wardrobe?'

'He doesn't like any of her clothes. Besides, she's dead.'

My father said it was a neat idea. 'You know she's entered for a ghost-story competition run by the Children's Library?'

'You put her up to that. Can't you see how wrong it is to encourage her to be so self-centred? Shut in the toolshed, scribbling, brooding. She has no fun, she has no friends, she won't mix, she just sits.'

'It's what she wants.'

'Have you thought what nasty habits it can lead to?'

A letter came for me, addressed to Miss Zephrine Pollock,

in a window envelope with the Borough arms on the flap. My mother opened it. Children don't get official letters and if they do, they can't be expected to deal with them. It was from the Chief Librarian, a man with initials after his name, informing Miss Pollock that she had won a prize in the ghost-story competition. She would be presented with a beautifully illustrated edition of Grimm's *Fairy Tales* at a ceremony in the Town Hall before local dignitaries and parents. The letter ended with the date and time of the presentation, congratulations, and best wishes for my continuing literary success.

My mother disapproved of the whole thing. Her wish was that no more should come of it because winning would give official sanction to my wrong ideas. She put the letter in the rack behind the gas bill.

My father found it. It was the last straw and it broke up their camel's-back marriage.

'This is addressed to Zeph.'

'Yes.'

'She hasn't seen it?'

'There's still time.'

'It means a lot to her, she's been watching and hoping for a letter. You must have known that.'

If they could have quarrelled they could have done it then. She could have, she was ready to rocket and explode.

He said, 'Shall you show her the letter, or shall I?'

'Shall you tell her I wouldn't?'

'This is for you,' he said to me.

When he left us he took nothing, not a toothbrush, not a shirt, just an old trilby and a snapshot of me from the photograph album, as I found out later. He wrote that she needn't worry about money, he would provide.

What seemed to upset her most was the thought of him buying new clothes, buying shaving-cream, toothpaste, hairbrush, slippers, pyjamas.

'What does he think we are? Infectious? Are his things dirty or shameful? Don't I wash and iron his shirts the minute he takes them off? Sponge his suits? Polish his shoes?'

I said perhaps he wanted a change and when he'd had it he'd come back.

14

'Do you think I'd have him back? Don't you get the message? He doesn't want anything I've touched!'

As it turned out, he left for less than a straw, because she took me to the presentation. She didn't tell me I was to be presented, but she made me put on my accordion-pleated tartan, and long white socks and patent strap shoes.

'Where are we going?' She tied back my hair with a ribbon. 'I look an absolute idiot,' I said.

'Try to look like a nice happy little girl.'

It wasn't true that I had no friends. I had Nell Peppiatt. Nell was not self-seeking, she sought other people. They need not feel they were letting themselves in for anything because she lived in a condition of friendship with everyone.

It was in our schooldays. One winter afternoon I stayed reading in the library. I liked school when I was alone in it. Walking along the empty corridors, I could watch myself reflected in the dark windows: Zephrine Pollock, the shape of things to come. I would use my full name, the one Mavis, my mother, had given me. It would grace any book jacket: *War and Peace*, *Wuthering Heights*, *Gone With the Wind*. By Zephrine Pollock.

There would be a commemorative plaque in the school hall, taking pride of place above the Distinguished Old Girls. I would be the most distinguished, my school essays preserved for posterity in a showcase. When the school got into financial difficulties they would be sold to an American university for thousands of dollars and the school would be saved. The trouble was, I'd have to be dead, memorabilia aren't worth much while you're alive and making new ones.

My image was blanked out by one of the lights in the corridor. I moved along to the next window. A flaw in the glass tended to lengthen my nose and narrow my hips and generally re-proportion me, which was heartening. A fattish girl does not look especially creative. But I hadn't realized that I was dull.

'To be boring is the worst social crime you can commit,' my mother had said.

'Do I bore you?'

'Of course not. You are my flesh and blood.'

15

There is this closed circuit whereby a parent can implant an unsatisfactory and displeasing system in a child and be smug about it. So far as looks were concerned I would have preferred to take after my father. His flesh and blood stayed within bounds; the bounds my mother kept were elasticated and foam-cupped. I worried that my body was going to end up S-shape, like hers.

I surprised Nell Peppiatt in Upper School cloaks. Actually, I was surprised, she wasn't. She had every right to be there. She was sixteen, idyllically pretty and socially successful. As different from me as chalk from cheese. I was prepared to accept the cheese identity but there was nothing chalky about Nell. She dazzled.

She had taken off the wall a framed instruction about not putting sanitary towels or foreign bodies down the lavatory pans (amended by someone to 'foreign babies') and laid it across one of the wash-basins. Set out on the board were jars, tubes, combs, tissues, tweezers, a hairbrush, nail varnish, ear-rings and a pair of pink silk gloves.

'Hi!' She welcomed the prospect of company.

I dived into a cubicle and bolted the door with what I intended to be finality. I wanted the encounter as brief as possible. Nell Peppiatt was enviable for all the wrong reasons. I ought not to be comparing myself with her and minding about the comparison, I ought to be thinking about Art.

On the lavatory I thought about the Venus de Milo, but then I started to worry about how she would manage a call of nature. A real artist would have risen above the surroundings, or turned them to creative advantage. I stood up and pulled the chain.

'Is Eff short for Effie?' Nell had her nose to the mirror, either she was shortsighted or she wanted to kiss her reflection.

'I suppose so.'

'Don't you know your own name?'

'My name's Zeph.'

'Is that short for Zephyr?'

'No, for Zephrine.'

Nell stretched her lips to apply lipstick. 'See if you can find my eyelash. I must have dropped it.'

'What?'

'On the floor.'

Incredulous, I looked, and found a whole string of eyelashes. She spread them on her palm. I said, 'Do they hurt?'

'Heavens, no. But you must get the balance right before you start fluttering.' When she stuck the things on her eyelid she put me in mind of a china doll, I fancied I could hear the glass eyes dropping into place. 'Don't go, little Breeze. Stay and talk.'

She turned to me with a flourish. The effect was dramatic. Gone was her bright electric prettiness, she was cherry-lipped and peach-skinned; her eyelids, coloured green and fringed with black, lowered and lifted to a slow heartbeat, getting the balance right. That too was Art, 'Nature's own sweet and cunning hand' hadn't laid it on.

She began heaping up her hair, she knew where to put each strand without looking at the mirror. She popped hair-clips in her mouth and spoke round them. 'How old are you?'

I lied. 'Fourteen.'

'And still in Lower School?'

'I'm backward.'

'You should do something about yourself.'

'Take extra lessons?'

'You've got grease pimples. Get a medicated soap and give your skin a good scrub. Your eyebrows are like hairy caterpillars.'

'Your eyelashes are like earwigs.'

'Swapping insults is childish. I'd like to help you.' She had her hair pinned on top of her head, a couple of ringlets falling with utmost artistry to either cheek.

'To do what?'

'Make the best of yourself. You've really let go.'

'I don't care.'

'I used to say that when I was your age. I was a bolster all the way down. I had a moustache when I stood in the sun.' She sighed. 'I didn't care but I lived to regret it.'

'I'm how I was born, I'll always be the same.'

'That's defeatist, which I wouldn't expect from you.'

It was news that Nell Peppiatt, classified in the school hierarchy as a 'young adult', attractive, smart, a social butterfly to my worm, had expected anything of me.

'It's what I am that matters.' I sounded smug.

17

'So what are you?'

'I've got to go.'

She seized me by the shoulders and turned me to the mirror. 'This is what you are.' I saw the same old face, white and shiny like a basin, with brown cook marks under the eyes, like the basin my mother cooked steak-and-kidney pudding in. 'Here's what you could be.'

She took my front fringe, swept it back from my forehead and fixed it with a band across my scalp. She moved fast and fearlessly. While I was still gaping at my naked face in the mirror she dipped her fingers into one of the pots and smeared something on my nose. I twisted my head aside.

'Hold still if you want to see a miracle.'

'I don't!'

'Mirror, mirror on the wall, who's the prettiest of us all?'

'*Fairest* – it's iambic pentameter. Stop putting muck on my face!'

'This muck as you call it, is blusher, non-clogging, super-covering, personally tinted. I think mulberry's right for you. Wait a minute and you'll get the surprise of your life.'

I found I was wedged with my back against the wash-basin while she rolled professional thumbs over my cheekbones. Short of shoving her bodily aside, which I couldn't bring myself to do, there was no escape from her ministrations. I tried dropping to my knees, she dropped with me.

'You must be blind as a bat trying to see through that fringe and these eyebrows. I'll tidy them up.'

'Plucking your eyebrows makes you go bald.'

'Who told you that?'

'My mother.'

'She's crazy. Hold still, I'll outline them and you'll get the general effect.'

'I don't want to look like a guy!'

'Do I look like a guy?'

'You look like a stranger.'

'I don't intend to keep the same face every day. Change your face, change your nature. Don't you want to be different?'

'I *am* different.'

'You've got a Cupid's bow. Did you know? Jungle Red brings

it out. The best of this is you can wash it off and be ready for something else. Of course we've each got our own type. Mine's romantic, I use lichen eye-shadow. You could do with something more intense – emerald sapphire. I see you as a *femme fatale*. Do get up off the floor.'

Getting up, I caught sight of a revelation in the mirror. Revealed was a black-browed creature, milky-skinned, with the forehead of a Tudor queen and a bandeau like a telephonist's headphones, except that where the ear-pieces would be were plastic rosebuds. She stared out of the mirror with coolness and a hint of malice, no one I knew, but she had been waiting under my skin like the flesh of a banana waiting to be peeled.

'What did I tell you? You're a different person. How does it feel?'

'Spooky. I'm going to wash it off.'

'How can you know how you feel about yourself until you know how other people feel about you?'

She might have half a point, but on the other hand, if I didn't care how other people felt about me I was in a better position to make up my own mind. 'I prefer the way I am.'

'Try it out before you decide.'

'Try what out?'

'Your new persona. I promise you you won't want to go back to being the Netball Nettie type.'

'I'm not!'

'It'll be fun, and instructive about the facts of life which they don't teach us in school.'

'We have sex instruction.'

'Old stuff. I knew it all before I knew my a b c, I picked up the basics from our cats. I'm talking about the spiritual thing.'

'I'm not religious.'

'I mean charisma. If you haven't got it you have to work at it. School doesn't know such a thing exists, they give us a smitch of education and turn us out as baby-factories.'

'I'm never going to have children.'

'Then if you don't mind me saying so, little Breeze, you've got to learn to handle yourself.'

She of course was handling herself and it was fascinating to see the different ways – like cut glass, like velvet, like an egg or a

time-bomb – and to speculate why. People said she was insin-
cere.

'I could give you a workout, but if you're too scared . . .' She
shrugged. 'You'll waste a lot of time trying to do it on your
own. You could end up with a totally wrong personality and
ruin your whole life.'

I spoke to the mirror. 'This isn't me.'

'You can't expect to get it right first time.' She swept her
paraphernalia into a clutch bag. 'Let's take a walk.'

'Like this?'

'Fling your coat over your shoulders, it looks more casual. I
can't do anything about your feet. Where did you get those
shoes? Don't tell me, your mother bought them.'

My black strap shoes, sensible shoes bubbling over the joint
of my little toe, rebuked me, saying we have not changed, we
cannot pretend, we are your own two feet, you stand upon us,
whoever you think you are. I watched them shoot out from
under my skirt, separate entities and unfriendly. They could be
working up to something.

'Stop walking like a penguin!'

'Where are we going?'

'Point your toes forward, walk on the balls of your feet –
you've got balls, you know.' Nell sniggered. The lewdness
didn't bother me, in school it was a fact of life. What I objected
to was the ugly sound coming from that pretty nose. 'Your
trouble is you're a mother's girl. It's written all over you.'

'You don't even know my mother.'

'No need. I can hear her: "Stop growing, stop having month-
lies and don't let me catch you with pubic hair, I want you to
be my little girl till death us do part." '

'It's not like that.'

'I was Daddy's girl.' Nell took my arm and penguin or not, we
walked in step. 'Daddy didn't mind me growing up and becoming
a woman so long as I was his sweetheart. He was jealous if I
looked at anyone else, he wanted to be the only man in my life,
he wanted me to adore him for ever and ever. Well, it wasn't on,
I had plans of my own and I told him so. He put me over his knee
and spanked my bottom. I bit through his sock to his ankle-bone,

20

whereupon he rushed off to get an anti-tetanus jab and his arm swelled up so he couldn't shave or sign his cheques.'

'Did he forgive you?'

'Forgive *me*? The boot was on the other foot. Fortunately he died.'

'Fortunately!'

'It was a happy release for us both. He couldn't bear not being the centre of my universe and I was past that sort of thing. We fought like cat and dog.'

'But you caused his death – biting and poisoning him –'

'Of course I didn't. His heart gave out, he was getting on for fifty-five.'

'What about your mother?'

'She's a merry widow.'

'Didn't she try to stop you fighting?'

'She used to slam the door and leave us to it.'

That was unimaginable. I couldn't imagine my mother and father acting like that. I had always assumed that theirs was the only course of action open to parents. Now I was being shown another, with the possibility of there being yet more. It was alarming because it showed how uninspired my outlook was. Inspiration, as I now realized, didn't necessarily uplift, it could go the other way, in fact it had to go every way under the sun and I must be receptive to all of them. I am, I am! I cried to myself.

Nell said, 'Stop jumping about, you look daft. Fourteen did you say you were? You act like five. Try to look sulky.'

'Miss Abercorn says I do.'

'Some people like the sulky look, it turns them on.'

'Miss Abercorn says it betrays an innate resistance to learning.'

'I'm not talking about Miss Abercorn, I'm talking about people who are going to be the best part of your life.'

'Who?'

'Men.'

It occurred to me that there was a gap of more than years between us, but I let it pass as requiring more attention than I could give at that moment. 'Where are we going?'

'Round the back of Tesco's.'

'Why not round the front?'

'Don't be such a drag! Come on.'

My arm hooked in hers, I went, remembering about the balls of my feet. A fine drizzle was falling, the rain caused the ends of Nell's hair to glisten like fine wire in the streetlights. She was swivelling from the hips, walking slowly, and to keep pace I was obliged to put out my feet with an arrested motion, like Mussolini's soldiers. I thought how ridiculous we must look, a couple of scarecrows, my mother would say. It raised the point – one of us was pretty, so how would she scare crows?

'Hold your head up so people can see you!'

I was hoping people wouldn't, and stared down at my feet. I knew by the smell when we reached the Wimpy. Someone said, 'Hi, Sensational.'

Nell brought us to a halt. 'Are you addressing me?'

Two boys were squatting on their haunches in the rain and eating out of boxes. 'Who else?' One of them had a pigtail, the other had shaved his head and had a baby fuzz round his jaw.

'I thought you were talking to my friend,' said Nell.

'Are you hungry?'

'It depends what you're offering.'

'We're not. If you want to eat you use money. We had to.'

'Your friend's a dog,' said the other boy.

'And you're a dog's dirt.' Nell swung me round and we went away along the street to the whoops and whistles of the boys.

'Now I know how I look to other people – like a dog!'

'Morons. Peasants. Scumbags. Let's pop into the bus station, the heel of my shoe's wonky.'

Elbow to elbow she skimmed us into the path of a number-nine bus. The bus shuddered and slewed sideways, the driver leaned out of his cab and shouted. Nell waved.

'You nearly had us run over!'

'If his reactions are so slow he shouldn't be in charge of a bus.'

Inside the bus station she sat on one of the benches. 'Look at this, a stiletto heel which couldn't pop a balloon.' She stretched out her leg, the shoe swinging from her toe. A man watched with interest. 'Comes apart when it's wet and cracks when it's dry.'

'Bad workmanship,' said the man.

She slipped off the shoe and handed it to him. 'Can you see the name? Tutti-Frutti or Rue de la Paix or something.'

'That's your answer.' He was looking at her, not the shoe. 'Stick to British goods and you can't go wrong.'

'Where can I get it mended? There are all-night discos and all-night burger-bars but you never hear of an all-night heel-bar.'

She laughed, not as she had laughed in school, with a snort, but prettily, musically. I saw that pleasing other people was a complex and demanding business, even a voice-change was required. No doubt there were other refinements which I wouldn't be able to supply, so what was I doing there with a face that wasn't my own in a situation of Nell Peppiatt's making?

'I'm going,' I said.

She caught my arm and gripped with surprisingly strong fingers. 'This is my friend Zephrine. Such an unusual name don't you think?'

'What's yours?' said the man.

'Oh ordinary, like me!' Nell's bell-like cadence was a wonder, I wondered what she could be thinking about to produce such a sound. 'We're looking for somewhere to dance. My friend waltzes divinely.'

'Let me fix that heel.'

'Oh I wouldn't put you to trouble! I'll be happy just to sit and watch her dance. Do you know anywhere there's real ballroom-dancing?'

'Korea', said the man, 'is where a lot of this foreign stuff comes from. There's no British Standards Institute to keep them up to scratch. Sweated labour's their way of life. How can you expect a proper job from people who live in paper houses?'

'Japanese,' I said.

'Eh?'

'Japanese live in paper houses.'

'German, is she?' he said to Nell.

'Why should she be?'

'With a name like Zeppeline, she couldn't be anything else.'

'You could use a hearing-aid,' Nell said sweetly.

'Can we go now?' Hearing myself ask, I feared it betrayed a

23

weak mind. I struck off Nell's grasp and marched away, pen-guin-style.

She ran after me. 'That man's not representative. Give your-self a chance.'

'A chance of what?'

'To be someone and amount to something.'

'It's not what I want to amount to.'

'You mean your mother wouldn't like it?'

'I can't go home looking like this.'

'You're scared of her, that's the truth of the matter.' Nell did not need to define truth, she just stuck the label on, whatever the matter. 'If you can't handle your own mother I don't see you handling yourself. You're a schmo.'

Schmo was our current in-word. The Upper School spoke it with disdain, little girls in their black regulation knickers screamed it in the gym when someone got stuck on the vaulting-horse.

'I must wash my face.'

'Okay, let's find a puddle.' I took out my handkerchief and scrubbed my cheeks. Nell said, 'Now you really look a schmo.'

I was to remember that evening with a sinking feeling which sank me to the same depth every time. I should have cut Nell Peppiatt out of my life then and there.

'Don't fret,' she said, 'you can wash at my place.'

She stopped to look into the window of a tobacconist's. I was obliged to wait for her. A man was also looking into the win-dow. Even when it became obvious that he was her reason for stopping I had no premonition. He wore a raincoat like other men, a tired old raincoat like my father's. He *was* my father.

Nell turned, thrust her arm through mine, anchoring me. She need not have, I was rooted to the spot. My father, who had been looking at Nell, saw who she was attached to. His eyes widened.

'Hallo,' said Nell. 'This is my friend Zephrine.'

He stood blinking, he blinks as if he's wearing steamy glasses. 'What are you doing here?'

'We're taking a stroll after a day of strenuous cerebral exer-cise. We're students.' Nell was like a cat demanding to be petted, bridling and ogling him. He was waiting for me to tell him what I had done to myself and why. If he had suspicions he put them aside, giving me the benefit of the doubt. I felt my lips draw back in a grimace. I knew they must be bloodied where I had rubbed them and I must look like a dog that has just killed something.

'She's very liberated,' said Nell, 'and I don't mean that old feminine stuff. Men are bread, and women are jam, and that's as equal as we'll get. Zeph has had to fight for her freedom, she had a repressed childhood.'

'Shut up!'

'She's got plenty of spirit and I think that's the first priority, don't you? Before beauty, before brains. Who wants a cold fish for a woman?'

It occurred to me that she was trying to sell me to my own father. My stomach turned, so did my heart, but when I looked into his eyes I saw a twinkle.

He said, 'It's a wet evening, may I buy you young ladies coffee?'

We were sharing a joke, he and I, and the joke was on Nell, on gleeful, triumphant, strikingly pretty Nell Peppiatt.

We went to McDonald's. Nell checked her reflection in the window as we entered. It was, of course, satisfactory. She seated herself on a stool and twined her legs knee over knee. He went to fetch the coffee.

'Well?'

'Do you know who he is?'

'I don't have to, I've proved my point.'

'What point?'

'That it pays to make the best of yourself.'

'Pays? For a cup of coffee? He picked you up, not me.'

'Look in the mirror and you'll see why. You ruined a perfectly good maquillage because you're scared your mother will see you.'

'That's not why he didn't pick me.'

'As a matter of fact it was me picked him. To show you. He's old and fuddy, but you can see it works.'

'He's not fuddy.'

'He seems decent, but you can't be sure. He could be a pervert or just ordinary, gets his kicks groping.'

Something came into my throat. I supposed it was gorge

rising and I ought to be itemizing the experience. But my blood was boiling too, I was in an emotional fix.'

Nell said, 'You've gone as red as a radish.'

He came with coffee on a tray. He had to rebuke some horsing boys who nearly knocked it out of his hands. They put up their fingers behind his back.

'Here we are.' He stooped to set out the cartons, a tall man with a composed face, when my mother raged it locked at the corners.

'You remind me of someone,' Nell said. 'A French film star, he keeps his pipe in his mouth and doesn't talk.'

'I don't smoke a pipe.'

'Jacques Tati. I like silent men. You haven't told us your name.' He smiled at her, his habitual gentle smile. 'I think names should be geared,' she said. 'You shouldn't label a child before you know how it's going to turn out. Look at Zeph, called after a puff of air, which makes her some sort of ninny.'

He was looking at her. 'What about you?'

Looking with him, I saw how the rain had served to enhance, yet blend the colours she had laid on her face. Drops sparkled in her hair. There was invitation in the way her lips parted and I saw where the invitation was directed.

'Me? I'm called after the heroine of a crappy novel my mother happened to be reading.'

'*Rebecca*?'

'That's a minor classic, a study of love and jealousy.' She spread one silver-tipped hand on the table. She did not add up to total absurdity, or to total anything. I sensed a discrepancy in her which was also an armament.

'Are you a Charles?' she said. 'A Henry? I know – you're a George. You have a Georgic face.'

'What sort of face is that?'

'Honest.'

She laughed, so did he. He rather overdid it, but as he rarely laughs he has no sense of proportion.

I said, 'I've got to go.'

They ignored me, they were on a private line and she was playing him over the rim of her coffee carton.

'Faces are fronts.'

He took the bait. 'Some more decorative than others.'

She, having every right, accepted the compliment with more than grace. She bunched her lips into a strawberry smile. 'Women make up to please men. And themselves. I use a dark make-up because I'd like to be a brunette.'

'It would be a pity.'

'I want to look enigmatic. Like Mona Lisa.'

'Rather a disagreeable lady.'

'My *mother*', I spoke up, 'will be worrying where I am.'

'Do you prefer blondes?' Nell said.

'I think you're very well as you are.'

'Would you say I'm mysterious?'

'No.'

'Just boring!'

'I didn't say that.'

They smiled into each other's eyes. He was obviously enjoying himself. I stood up, rocking the table and spilling my coffee which I hadn't touched. He sighed and reached for his hat.

'You're not going?' cried Nell.

'I'm going home,' I said.

'I'm sorry,' he said, 'it's getting late and her mother will be concerned.'

'*You* don't have to go –'

'I'll see her home.'

'She's coming home with me.'

'It's rather too late for that. I shouldn't like her walking home alone afterwards.'

'I'll walk her home.'

'Then you would have to return alone.' He settled his hat squarely on his head. 'I wouldn't like that either.'

'She can stay the night – we've already arranged it.'

'Have you?' he said to me.

'No.'

'Zeph – you mustn't go with him!'

I walked away.

Next morning she came into Lower School cloaks as I was changing. 'What happened? Did he try anything?'

'Of course not.'

She plumped herself down on my locker, prepared to be weighty. 'You know what I think? I think you didn't even realize what he was after. I think you thought you were just being walked home.'

'Excuse me, I have to change my shoes.'

'That sort of ignorance amounts to criminal negligence on the part of someone. You're a criminal négligée!'

'Let me get to my locker. We have gym first lesson.'

'Didn't your mother ever tell you not to go with strange men?'

'He's not strange, she's married to him.'

'What?'

'He's my father.'

'Your *father*?' The effect was all I could have wished. But only momentarily. Instead of deflating, Nell rose to the occasion and demolished it. 'Really? Your old man? You're smarter than I thought.'

'The whole thing was dead stupid.'

'Does he make you play games?'

'He doesn't make me do anything.'

'Mine did. We played Hunt-the-Slipper and Adam-and-Eve-and-Pinch-Me. It was pretty harmless.' Nell sighed. 'Poor old dad got something out of it.'

I realized that I had to decide whether to believe her, I would always have to do that, it would be a question of judgement – mostly snap. The question was, did I want such a troublesome friendship.

The question did not survive because she saw me in particular terms, not merely the general state of friendliness she offered to everyone. I suppose it was the attraction of opposites. There must be people even more opposite than me, but she made the choice and left me none.

She championed my ambitions, discounting Miss Abercorn who at that time was my only mentor. 'The woman's a quack.'

'She's read James Joyce.'

'Old Norse stuff.'

'James Joyce is Irish.'

'She's paid to teach us *English* literature.'

' "Use your imagination," she said to the class, "give it free rein, write whatever comes into your heads, let's see what those nubile minds of yours can do." I looked up nubile and it means marriageable, sexually attractive.'

28

'Which she never was.'

'I wrote four and a half pages and she called me out. "What's all this", she said in front of everyone, "about seas and surges and swelling billows and fickle moons?" "It's a noctuary," I said, "a record of night thoughts." "Whose, may I ask," she said. "The Lady of Shalott's," I said, "she had a fever in her blood." "What gave you that idea?" she said. "My imagination," I said. She said, "Go and wash it out." '

'What was the Lady of Shalott thinking?'

'Alone on that island with nothing to do but weave she'd be bound to have ideas she couldn't admit to. She'd sit and watch the river in her mirror and she'd think of being drawn down into the embrace of the sea and drowning with fishes in her hair and seaweed caressing her limbs.'

Nell laughed. 'Hot stuff.'

'I got minus D.'

'Don't let that worry you.'

'Miss Abercorn doesn't like *Ulysses* either, she says it's immensely flawed.'

'There you are then.'

I cried, 'I'm not! I'm nowhere!'

'She's jealous.'

'Of James Joyce?'

'Of you. She's never had anything published.'

'Nor have I.'

'You will,' Nell said confidently. 'Who's going to print the grot she writes?'

'She's writing a history of the Brontës.'

'The Brontesaurus.'

'I'll ask her how she would have described the Lady of Shalott's thoughts.'

'She won't know, she's got no blood to have a fever in.'

It was easy for Nell to joke, but I feared Miss Abercorn. She ringed my words and underscored whole sentences with her blue pencil. 'Really!' she wrote, large across the page.

'Please,' I said when we were alone, the rest of the class had gone and she was wiping present indicatives off the blackboard, 'What's wrong with my essay?'

'Wrong?' Bristles marshalled on her lip, causing my heart to sink. 'I abhor the symbolism and the thinking behind it. Not your thinking, Pollock, because you didn't pause to do any. You picked up the old insult out of the dust where it belongs and proclaimed it in what I can only call Della-Cruscan style.'

'Does that mean poetic?'

'It means euphuistic and sentimental.'

'What I thought was, the Lady of Shalott just sitting there at her loom all day and all night, saw the lovers going to Camelot and wished there was someone special for her. And it being a poem I thought I ought to keep it poetic, sort of glorify what she was feeling.'

'You glorified a lie, the slander perpetuated throughout history for the advantage of mankind. *Man* –' Miss Abercorn exploded the word – 'is a generic term. The sole provision made for women is as a sub-specie, the side issue of Adam's rib. The inference being that a woman has nothing better to do than wait for a man. And the most she can hope for, the ultimate accolade, is that as he passes her by he may notice that she is beautiful.' Miss Abercorn's cheek mottled with whatever served her for blood. 'I refuse to subscribe to the myth of the weaker vessel. Humanity is split in two and therein lies its undoing.'

I thought it an interesting proposition with a lot to be said on both sides. I put my question, 'How would you have done it?'

'I would not have created the sexes.'

'I meant, how would you have described what the Lady of Shalott felt?'

Miss Abercorn picked up her keys. 'I wouldn't presume. Come along, Pollock, I have to lock up.'

After I left school I went to work for a firm of debt collectors. I thought they could have found an easier way to make a living, I thought that before I went to work for them. It was out of a sort of whimsicality, and because their premises were near our house that I applied for the job.

Of course they have ways of getting money out of people. They start polite, letters begin 'Dear Sir', under a discreet heading – 'Credit Control Service', no mention of debts. (Writing to a Japanese gentleman once, I took it on myself to address him as 'Honoured Sir', but they said that was going too far.)

I type the credit reports and make the tea. Mr Ginsberg does company searches and mortgages. Mrs Ginsberg deals with vehicle reclamations and arrears of hire purchase and TV rentals. Mr Ginsberg wears dark glasses which give him a useful dangerous look and hide the fact that he has watery eyes. Any sign of weakness is bad for the business. Mrs Ginsberg told me that one of the reasons she decided to engage me was because I looked strong. Mr Ginsberg has the front office and the biggest desk, but she's the brains of the firm, not so much an *éminence grise* as an *éminence* avocado, she wears green tweed suits and yellow cardigans.

The day after my seventeenth birthday I found my father waiting outside the office. He was wearing the old trilby which was one of the few things he took with him when he left. It bends his ears down.

He tried to kiss me. I turned my face aside. 'I brought your birthday present. It's pocket-size so you can carry it with you.'

It was in a W.H. Smith's bag, a concise dictionary. 'Thanks,' I said. 'Are you coming back to us?'

'I wanted to be in touch.'

'You could have written.'

'Does she still open your letters?'

'You could have written to her.'

'I want you to have my address.'

'What for?'

'In case you need me.'

'What shall I tell her?'

'I think – better nothing.'

'I don't expect she'll want to see you. It's been years.'

'It's been a hard time.'

Looking him over as I would a stranger, which he was, I saw that he was fatter but his hair was thinner. He was starting a beard, or he hadn't shaved.

'Are you still going to be a writer?'

'Of course.'

'Bravo.' He spoke as to the child I was when he left, twelve years of age, without a clue about the art of writing, turning out little stories about beautiful heiresses and wicked stepmothers. 'If there's anything I can do to help –'

'There isn't. Writing's something you have to do alone. I help myself by reading other people's books. Not for their ideas, for their mistakes. I don't intend to make the same ones.'

'If I change my digs I'll let you know.'

'Why did you go away?'

'Because I wasn't doing any good.'

I took that to mean he had been doing harm, it wasn't reason enough otherwise. 'I could prepare her if you like.'

'What for?'

'To take you back.'

'I don't want to come back, but I don't want to lose you.'

I might have said he had already lost me, but I don't know if that's true, I don't know if we can ever be rid of one another. 'What about her?'

'Will you let me know if you go away?'

'You didn't let me know.'

'That was a different case.'

Later he wrote that he had moved to Sydenham. 'Come and see us,' he wrote. He wasn't one to use the plural pronoun out of matiness. Out of curiosity I went to the address.

A young man opened the door. He was tall enough for his head to touch the lintel, broad-shouldered and slim-hipped, the colour of bitter chocolate. He was a surprise, I'd expected a woman.

'Is Mr Pollock in?'

'Whom shall I say is enquiring?'

'His daughter.'

He raised his brows, causing three symmetrical tucks to appear in his satin forehead. 'Miss Zeph, I presume?'

I was ushered into a passage and then into a room where my father was reading a newspaper. He stood up as he always did when anyone came or went, unfailingly polite my mother said, and held it against him.

'I thought you'd like to have this.' As my reason for coming I had brought his camera, one of the few things of his which she hadn't thrown away.

'It's yours, I gave it to you.'

'I've got a new one, it prints the pictures as soon as I've taken them.'

'A polaroid snap camera, what they used to call an Insta-matic,' said the young man.

My father said, 'This is Maria's brother.'

'Maria?'

'Montrose Odenda.' The young man actually clicked his heels. He wore white kid platform shoes and a business suit. His hair was pure wool, tightly curled. He had minuscule ringlets in each nostril. He said, 'Will you take tea?'

'I'm not staying, I came to bring the camera.'

'I'd like you to meet Maria,' said my father.

'Another time.' I twitched two fingers to him and turned to the door.

The young man slipped into the passage with me. 'You'll come again?'

'I don't know.'

'You're his family.'

'I didn't leave him, he left me.'

I did go back a few days later, mainly for the purpose of extending my range to Montrose Odenda. I was curious about him and whether he connected with my father's childhood. But the next time a girl came to the door. She wore a pink dress with built-up shoulders and her skin was like a nugget of coal. She had had her hair straightened, pulled up to the crown of her head and pushed through a rubber band.

'Is Mr Pollock at home?'

'Not this minute.'

'What about the next one?' She could be pert, so could I.

'Maybe the one after.'

'Can I come in and wait?'

'Are you from the Council?'

'I've come to see my father.'

She opened up a dazzling row of teeth. 'Come and sit down.'

'I'm not staying.'

'That's what you said before.'

'Before what?'

'When you came before. You weren't staying you said, he told me, he saved up every word you said. You're his lovely child.' She was twinkling, she was one who would twinkle all over, the Maria he wanted me to meet. 'Why don't you come and visit him?'

'I'm here now.'

'You took your time – you took his time and he doesn't have so much as you.'

'It's really none of your business.'

'That man's my business.'

I thought she should be more careful. Black or white, it doesn't recommend anyone to answer before the question has been asked.

We were in the kitchen. The walls were emulsioned bright blue, there was a green bird in a birdcage and the stone sink and brass tap are sold as bygones in trendy shops.

'Take off that nice coat,' she said. 'You can't sit to tea in it. Take it through the beads.'

The beads hung on strings from an arch. When I touched them they clicked slyly, letting me into a secret. In the room beyond, the double bed was unmade, the clothes heaped, the pillows had last night's hollows in them. I stood and thought this is where – remembering the bed at home when he was home and they had just got out of it, and Mrs Spilsbury's bed, and Toplady's bell-push chin. I wasn't being coherent but I didn't have to be – it was a lesson in how to write about sex without mentioning it.

On the dressing-table I saw a comb with black hairs in the teeth, black wire hairs. In the wardrobe were a jacket, a raincoat the colour of brown paper, her dresses the colours of the rainbow, and a leopard-spot coat. No secret.

I broke through the beads and she said, 'You didn't take your coat off.'

'Does your brother live here with you?'

'Don't get him on your mind, he only cares about his books.'

'Books?'

'He talks about Austen and Bacon – bacon's a book? – says the Bible's the paperback of Moses's tablets.'

'Is he a writer?'

'He's godless. Put him out of your mind, child.'

'I'm not a child, I'm as old as you are. Perhaps older.'

34

'You were nurtured. I raised myself, and half a dozen kids as well. Had to be a year ahead all the time.'

'I'm seventeen.'

'I've still got those extra years, reckon I'm going on for thirty!'

She heard, I didn't, the sound of the street door opening. She ran into the passage. My father came into the kitchen with her laughing and jumping to get her arms round his neck. He hadn't had time to remove his hat and she knocked it sideways.

I was searching for my prose style – radiant, crisp, bold, powerful, trenchant, pithy, deep, distinctive – never to be confused with any other. But someone had always got there first, got the words on the page: some radiant, some pithy, some powerful, many deep, but none of them was everything I wanted. I have flashes of brilliance, I wanted a conflagration.

Mavis Pollock had no notion that her daughter was out of the ordinary. Although there were early unmistakable signs of the genius which has now matured and won world-wide acclaim, they were unrecognized . . .

She thought I was shutting her out. I was, because she had no place in my creativity. She would come into my room when I was working.

'Doesn't it ever occur to you that I would like company? Someone to talk to? Nothing heavy, just how was your day.'

She was good at putting me in the wrong. I suppose that's a sort of gift.

'Perhaps you'd like to hear about *my* day. I'm not saying it was more exciting than yours, but things happened.'

I covered my notes, I never leave them exposed, I would sooner expose my body privates, these are the privates of my mind, without even a shell of bone to protect them.

She said, 'Cousin Gladys sends you her love.'

'You've been to Sydenham?'

'I saw the Creature.'

'Maria Odenda?'

'What else do you know about her?'

My notes were in a folder but I was afraid they might not be the same after this. 'It doesn't matter.'

'Are you telling me that part of my life doesn't matter?'

'Maria's not your life.'

'She's living with my husband, the man I lived with for fifteen years, it makes her part of my life. The worst part.'

Maria had said he was *her* business. Women tie themselves to men. It doesn't work both ways, if men tied themselves to women the system would break down. I'm going to have to write about the system.

'I want to know why. Why her? A black African!'

'She's British.'

'How can she be!'

'She was born in this country. She's never been outside England. Her parents took work on a ship and never came back, so her brother brought her with him to do his washing and cleaning. He doesn't mind having my father live with them.'

'I wouldn't have cared if he'd taken a woman, any woman, she didn't even have to be white, but that . . .' her lip trembled as it curled, 'that piccaninny!'

'She's as old as me.'

'Of course you talk to her, to her and your father and the brother – you tell them what you've been doing.'

'Let's go and have supper.'

'Do you tell them about me?'

'There's nothing to tell.'

'Of course not. Naturally your father fancies black girls, he was brought up with them.'

'It's not what you'd call love.'

'What would I call it?'

'You mustn't feel bad about it.'

'Of course not. It doesn't matter, does it?'

'What you're going through does.'

'I'm not going through anything on his account. In the beginning, yes, I went through it all. Love, yes, I'd call it that, I don't want you to think you were born of a loveless marriage. But it's over now and I don't care that he's sleeping with a golliwog.'

'What did you see when you went to Sydenham?'

'I saw the black girl drop her shopping in the street.'

'Anything else?'

'I saw him coming and I left.'

'It wasn't so much, was it?'

'I'm well aware that Gladys derives entertainment from watching what goes on across the street and she expected to be more entertained watching me watch. I made up my mind not to give her the satisfaction. I thought I might manage not to have any feelings.

'Gladys had prepared what she called a cold collation, a pork pie and pickled onion each, to take upstairs on a tray. I asked if such a vigil was necessary. She said they came home at midday and I'd be able to see the girl. That's what you want, isn't it, she said – to see his girl? I said what he did was no longer any concern of mine, but that what *you* saw was. Gladys said you go into the house, talk to them and eat with them. Heaven knows what you see, she said. I said it's what Zephrine thinks of them, may be led to think, that concerned me. Gladys said it was better not to know, it would only upset me.

'Gladys has been advised to rest in preparation for surgery. She rests in a chair at her bedroom window. She had her knitting, a transistor, a pair of opera glasses and a jar of extra strong mints. We could watch what went on while we ate our lunch, she said. I went to a theatre matinée once and we had tea on trays.

'Gladys pointed out their house. It has a yellow gate, she said he'd spent a Sunday morning painting it. I didn't like sitting there with a pie and a pickled onion on a plate, in front of her window with the curtains looped back as if ready for a show. There was a manhole cover which clattered every time a car went over it. The noise would drive me crazy. I expect he painted the gate yellow to remind him of Jamaica. But of course he has the piccaninny to do that. Gladys says she will never understand why I don't divorce him.

'Someone behaving like a windmill came along the street. As she got nearer I saw that she was swinging a shopping bag round her head. She had on an orange shift and white sneakers. The bag suddenly flew out of her hands and landed on the pavement. Brown liquid bubbled out. The girl put her hands on her hips and watched it. Gladys said it was the beer for his supper and the girl was his black Maria. I said she looked little more than a child. They mature early, Gladys said, at night their appetites are aroused and she's seen them romping.

'The girl went into the house, leaving broken glass scattered over the pavement. I said I couldn't stay, I'd just seen him coming, my legal husband with a life unknown to me, but guessed at. I can guess at it all!'

I said, 'You mustn't let your imagination run away with you.' It's what she's always telling me.

Another letter from Nell.

> *Liebchen*, prepare yourself. You are to become an auntie, the old-fashioned sort, not a poove. I think I'm pregnant – hell, I know I am. It's been confirmed. I went to a doctor and was tested. I'll tell you about that when I see you, I'm not putting it on paper. It's no wonder doctors get struck off for poking their women patients. Where does one thing stop and the other begin?
>
> Boris has a commission for our landlady, Mrs Trompetto. She said we could live rent-free if he did a prancing horse for her yard. Boris has never done a horse and he can't get the prance right. He got it standing up, its front legs in the air, it looked like a prize-fighter. Next morning it was on the floor and it looked like a rockery. Boris cried.
>
> He's so big and hairy, yet he bawls like a baby. I don't think I can cope with two bawlers. If his work goes wrong, everything's wrong. I said the cat might have jumped on it and he cried it was himself lying there in pieces, as a creative artist he was broken up. He'd better not be, we can't pay the rent. I tell Mrs Trompetto her horse is coming along fine.

There was more about Boris, Boris as an artist, a man, a wooer, a sensitive spirit, a beloved vagabond, a home-lover. 'He wants to make me a birthing stool. I said, *Chéri*, I'm not going to sit up peeling potatoes while this child is being born. Where Boris comes from it's the father's first gift to the mother of his child. He says it's traditional. Can you imagine?'

She had added a postcript: 'Ran out of paper, so had to use the back of a Shrink Yourself correspondence course.'

I turned the letter over. What seemed to be part of a questionnaire was printed on the other side:

Identify your tingle factor. Is it music? Poetry? Nature – specify which aspect: speleology, baroque art, animals, babies, nude studies? Do you achieve a positive arousal with selective chastisement?

Is your body clock on time? Retarded? Advanced?

Do you have ejaculatory fantasies? Does your bust disappoint?

In what way – size, shape, reactivity? (Delete as inapplicable.)

Describe your parents as briefly as possible. (Do not write in the margins. If you need more space attach another sheet. No staples, please.)

Have you been fair?

Do you subscribe to (a) the Big Bang theory? (b) a wine club? (c) book clubs?

Would you like to change your gender?

What is your earliest memory?

I started filling it in as an exercise in getting to know myself. I identified my tingle factor as literature. Selective chastisement I supposed meant good hiding and wrote 'Of course not'.

To the question about a body clock, I replied 'Not known', but about ejaculatory fantasies I do know. I am often moved to exclaim aloud, groan, or sigh about mine.

I have never been pleased with my bust. 'Too big and I don't intend to use it.'

The next injunction was a challenge. Eight lines were allotted, four to each parent. 'Edgar Pollock, my father,' I wrote, and sat twiddling the form. I have never considered committing either of my parents to paper. Where to start? 'He is tall but not handsome, his hair is brown. He is not good' – I crossed out 'good' and wrote 'bad'. He does what he thinks is good but it turns out bad.

'My mother has dark hair and grey eyes and is a good cook.'

That was fair enough, as far as it went. I experienced a strong reluctance to go any farther.

The next section was straightforward. I did not know what the Big Bang theory was and answered 'No'.

Given the option, I would not choose to be female. I find it restricting, but it is also a challenge. The drawbacks have to be utilized to bring forth words that are purer, stronger and rarer than men with all their advantages can produce.

To the last question on the sheet I replied 'OXO'. My earliest memory is of writing the word in infant school. We had been asked to think of three-letter words. 'Dog, cat, mat' were public property, what everyone wrote. OXO was my own, I was enchanted by its appearance on paper because backwards and upside down it remained the same. I multiplied it – OXOXOX-OXOXOXO – and was scolded for not paying attention.

In fine weather I take my lunch to the shopping precinct. The precinct is furnished with concrete logs. They're quite realistic if you accept concrete trees. Each log has whorls and cracks like bark and is whimsically carved: 'Tony loves Sharon', 'We woz here', and hearts pierced by arrows. Each log has the self-same whorls and the same inscriptions. I checked. Children plug chewing-gum into the letters while they wait for their mothers to come out of Sainsbury's.

Sometimes I go into Rizzio's, a coffee-bar. It's small and gets crowded at lunchtime. I was standing drinking my coffee when a gloved hand beckoned to me. It turned out to be the hand of Montrose Odenda, black and slender, with a pink palm.

He was at a table at the back of the room. When a girl tried to take the vacant chair by his side he pulled it to him, shook his head. The girl, who was pretty, lightly touched his hair, then dusted her fingers. He smiled.

When I could get to his table I said, 'I don't mind standing.'

'I mind talking up to you. Please sit.'

'I have to be back in the office by two.'

'May I buy you a doughnut?'

'No thanks.'

'Your father misses you. You haven't been to see him lately.'

'No.'

'Is it because of us, Maria and me?'

'I'm busy.'

'Doing what?'

'Writing. I'm a writer.'

It was the first time I had said it. Not 'I want to be a writer, I'm going to be a writer', but 'I *am* a writer'. Here in this ordinary place, among ordinary people, on a day like any other, the certainty hit and winded me. Of course I am a writer, always have been. It's in my bones, I have writing bones, I am a writer or I am nothing. Until that moment I had not declared it in public.

Montrose Odenda was, like me, extra-ordinary. Unlike me, he started from outside, the colour of his skin, his gold bracelet, pin-striped suit, dazzling white shirt and the peacock feather in his button hole were extra.

'I'm at work all day,' I said. 'I don't get much time to write.'

'What do you work at?'

'Debt collecting.'

'Strong human interest.'

Certainly there are some emotive moments in our office. There's nothing more emotive than money, Mrs Ginsberg says.

'Are you a writer?' I said.

'Why do you ask?'

'Maria says you only care about your books.'

'I'm taking a course in the appreciation of English literature. Your greatest achievement.'

'It will be.'

'It is already your countrymen's: Chaucer's, Hardy's, Dickens's, Trollope's, not to mention Shakespeare's. I don't aim to write, but to my way of thinking literature is the art form in which the English excel and I want to be able to converse on aspects of the novel, poetry and drama. I go to evening classes. Right now we are studying the work of W. Somerset Maugham. You will have read *A Writer's Notebook*.'

'No.'

'You could learn from that man.'

'I have to find my own words.'

'Where are you looking for them?'

41

'In books.'

'Which books? Will you write like Dylan Thomas? Or Jackie Collins?'

'I shan't write like anyone. My words have got my name on them.'

'Do you never worry that everything worth writing has been written?'

'Not the way I shall write it.'

He nodded. 'That is true of course. May I read something of yours?'

'When the words come right.'

Mavis, my mother, said to the telephone: 'Oh, it's you. I've been wondering how you are. Was it today the doctor . . . oh, yesterday. What's the matter? Has something happened? . . . Don't shout, I can't hear if you shout. Calm down. . . . What? A hat? . . . A *cat*? . . . Are you sure? . . . How beastly!' She turned to look at me. 'How perfectly beastly! . . . Don't be ridiculous, of course there's nothing in it. You're being silly . . . Stop that . . . how can I hear what you're saying if you . . . You know what they're doing, don't you? They're trying to upset you by making a nuisance. It's only what you can expect of people like that – No, I can't come over, what would be the point? Pull yourself together and ring the police. . . . Yes, the police, let them deal with it, it's what we pay rates for.'

She dropped the receiver with a gesture of distaste. 'Gladys is being persecuted by those friends of yours.'

'What friends?'

'I don't know what this country is coming to when a respectable white woman is persecuted in her own home by illegal immigrants.'

'Illegal?'

'I thought Gladys had more common sense than to let that sort of thing upset her.'

'What sort of thing?'

'Didn't they tell you? I thought you were in their confidence. Get your father to tell you, it will seem quite natural to him.'

She wouldn't say any more. I thought I'd better warn them that Gladys might send for the police. Besides, I wanted to

42

know what it was that was natural to my father and beastly to my mother.

He was pleased to see me. 'I knew you'd come.'

Maria was happy for him. 'He's been wish-wishing for you.'

'I can't come often.'

'You're his family, you have the biggest piece of him. But he never did use up all his heart, there's some left for me.'

'You know that someone's watching you?'

'Watching us?'

Maria shrugged. 'An old lady looks through spy-glasses.'

'You should be more careful.'

'We do nothing to be ashamed of. I fixed her.'

'What have you done?'

'Put a cat's tail through her letter-box.'

'*What*?'

'It's reckoned to bring bad luck. But the cat that's got no tail to wrap itself in is the unlucky one.'

'It's horrible.'

'White people scare as easy as black. Anyway, it wasn't a real cat, it was the tail of my old fur neckpiece.'

'Look,' I said, 'she's all alone and she's very upset.'

'Got to rattle the cans to scare the crows.'

'It's Cousin Gladys,' I said to my father. 'She lives across the street and she watches you from her window.'

Maria cried, 'You mean to say that old lady's your auntie's daughter?'

'She's my mother's cousin, my grandmother's sister's daughter. My mother was here and she watched too.'

'*She* came?' I always thought his face was boneless, suddenly it was knuckle-hard.

'Gladys is going to the police.'

'There's no law I know of against loving and touching,' said Maria. 'They pass it and we all go to jail. Nobody twisted her arm to keep looking if she didn't like what she saw.'

'I don't know what she saw.'

'Me posing maybe.'

'Posing?'

'I get tired to death of still lives, I wanted to do a nude. It had to be my own self, I can't afford a model. You think I

43

should know how I look? I never could draw from memory, so there I was, in front of that big mirror, naked to my birth-button, sketching.'

'You're an artist?'

'Just about the best painter in the world.'

'I don't see any of your pictures.'

'They're not allowed indoors. Montrose won't allow them. If your daddy can spare you for two minutes, I'll show you.'

She bustled me out to the yard. There was an out-house, the door slung on one hinge. She hitched it wide with her shoulder.

'Edgar fixed this place. Everything is here. I can throw paint, throw a fit, throw what I like.'

When she switched on the light, my first sensation was that someone was putting pressure on my eyeballs. I blinked, dazzled, in that confined space. It was chock-full of colour, solid greens and banana yellow, cover-girl red, sugar-bag blue, all daubed on wood, some of the wood mere boards, some whole packing-cases painted on top, sides and probably on the bottoms too. Paintings were stacked along the crossbeams of the roof. I found I was looking up at a spread eagle, or it could be a winged angel – Maria making her own Sistine chapel.

'I can smoke.' She proffered a tin with some hand-rolled cigarettes.

'Pot?'

'You crazy? Where would I get the money?'

She hung a cigarette on her generous lip. 'Contrary to what your cousin thinks, we're ordinary people.' She used the word as if it was the one she wanted to be identified by. 'I've no plans to set the world on fire, it's going to burn okay without me.' She struck a match on one of the paintings.

I could see a lot of paint, and smell it, layers and ridges and scabs of paint, some of it on wood so rough that splinters had broken through and stood out as coloured bristles. I looked for a real picture. I bent down, stretched up, looking. I touched a crudded whorl and my fingers were led to the middle of a maze.

'This – people running away from a rainstorm –'

'That's no rainstorm, that's Anansi, the Spider, smartest of all the animals in the forest.'

44

I wondered if she was aware that her paintings were junk and she was laughing at me. On the other hand, she might be serious, striking a match on her work could be a danger signal.

I said, 'I don't quite see where you're going.'

'Going the way I see things.'

'Do you only see colour?'

She reached under a bench and pulled out a sheet of cardboard. 'My first nude.'

It came as a surprise after the oils. It had shapes, a triangle of circles, the two lower ones with blobs in the centre, they might be eyes except that they were bigger than the circle at the apex which had a vertical line which might be a nose, and finger-rings round it which might be hair.

'Charcoal's a nice flesh tint. You can see it's me, can't you?'

'Why doesn't Montrose like your pictures?'

'He says it would be quicker to shoot me.'

'Don't you mind?'

'I don't mind him, he helps pay the rent.' She pinched out her cigarette. 'We had a hard time when we were children, he's going to give everyone a piece of it now.'

'I liked talking with him.'

'We lived with Aunt Luella Rigby. She had twelve children, she was one big womb. I took care of the little ones and Montrose was sent to buy meat. Aunt Luella taught him to choose the best and it had to be the cheapest too. Ask for the high-up cuts, she said, and when they're taken down you say that's too dear and if the man's lazy he'll take down the price sooner than reach up to hang them again. When we had chicken, Montrose had to pluck and gut them before he went to school. After school there was a list of jobs waiting, he never had a free minute. If you didn't please her, Luella gave you a hiding. Her arm was like the hind-kick of a mule.

'One day Montrose had no luck at the market. He brought back string and bones and she got ready to beat him. He was sixteen years old and skinny, but he took her up as gently as a mother taking up her baby and sat her on the stove. The stove was kept red hot because Luella felt the cold. When she jumped off she was scorched on both cheeks.'

Maria patted her chest to digest her laughter. My father had followed us and was in the doorway. 'So you told her where we live?'

'No, Gladys did.'

'Why didn't you tell me she was coming?'

Maria said, 'Her mamma was all set to see the show.'

'She didn't see anything,' I said.

'Nothing to grieve for?' Maria grinned.

He said, 'Why did she come?'

'Because of Gladys. She tries to stir things up. You won't stop her by putting things through her letter-box.'

'All I did was put one thing,' said Maria.

'She says you put messes on her doorstep and dig up her flowers.'

'Honey, there are dogs in this street.'

'She says you make degrading marks on her fence.'

'Dogs lift their legs and make degrading marks everywhere.'

'Your mother –' he spoke as if he didn't want her on his tongue, 'I can't go through that again.'

'You don't have to. She doesn't want you back.'

Maria said, 'A child can't know what goes on between man and wife.'

'I won a literary award and she hid the letter. After that he went away.'

'But you got your prize,' he said, 'and everyone clapped. *She* clapped. I was there, I kept out of sight, but she doesn't need eyes to see me.'

'Honey, don't let it get to you,' Maria said to him.

'You know why she came? It was to see you and me together.'

Because what she calls love was operating her, operating on him. And me. If we'd been a big family it would have pulled her apart.

'She wants me to give evidence,' I said, 'witness against you.'

'You can't be a witness, you haven't witnessed anything.'

'Look,' I said, 'you really scared Gladys, she can't sleep, she listens for every sound, worries about what you'll do next.'

Maria giggled. 'She only has to ask us.'

Certain words are prismatic. When I turn the pages of Chambers they signal to me: words like quiddity, belvedere, galactic, scrofulous, I'll have a lot of use for scrofulous. All I have to do is pick them out and get them in the right order and that will be my prose style. Miss Abercorn said it was Della-Cruscan, so it can't have been bad.

I'm working through other styles, sifting out the coarser parts, that's what Della-Cruscan means. My style will be pure grain.

Criticism is superfluous, her pages are redolent with beauty, drama, suspense. Sensitive, vibrant, poignant, deeply significant, here is Art of the highest order. Zephrine Pollock is Woolf, Murdoch and the Brontës in one. She has the strength of Hemingway and her plots are as masterful as Le Carré's, she is unputdownable. With this, her first novel, she takes her place among the literary giants. With her next she will overtop them all.

When the weather's too cold or wet to eat outside I take my sandwiches into Rizzio's. Smoking, spitting, eating your own food is strictly forbidden on the premises. I have ways of eating unseen. I put a sandwich in my hankie and pretend to be blowing my nose, or hold my notebook in front of my face. I take my exercises along in hope of seeing Montrose.

He found me half under the table, chewing on a Mars bar. 'Miss Zeph.' He was wearing a purple polo sweater, sharkskin trousers and accessories – gold chain bracelet, platinum wristwatch and a signet ring big enough to signet Magna Carta.

'I'm tying my shoelace.' I tried to shift the Mars bar off my teeth.

'Allow me.' He went down on one knee. People turned to look, someone laughed. 'Miss Zeph, your shoes have no laces.'

Seeing him smiling up at me, people thought he was proposing. A woman got annoyed and threw a bread roll.

'Please get up, people are looking.'

He rose with one graceful movement and indicated the chair facing me. 'May I?'

I was handicapped by my lunch in my lap. While he went to fetch his lunch I swallowed the last of the Mars bar and got my

Feint-Ruled Student's Second Year Notebook out of my hand-bag. I'd already filled the First Year Notebook which has fewer pages and no conversion tables.

He brought sandwiches and offered me one. I said I'd eaten. He opened up a sandwich, took out the meat and slipped it into the bread of another. 'Who was it said he couldn't eat anything that had a face?'

'That did,' I said. 'It's ham.'

'It's polyunsaturated fat compressed and flavoured with meat extract. There's only the ghost of a face here.' He bit into the double frill of pink.

I was thinking that his face was solid chocolate, you can't look far into that. 'Will you read something I've written?'

'Did the words come out right for you?'

'I don't know. I'm experimenting with styles. Mine will be new and completely different, these are just exercises.'

But when he took up my notebook I panicked. It was as if I'd betrayed a trust – not mine, something's much bigger and all-important. Art's.

He started to read, his lips moved, cushioning my words. He looked at me over the page: ' "Like from like recedes, conspicu-ousness drifts away . . . "?'

'Life from life – consciousness drifts away.'

' "Gigantic angels tumble like poppies in the emporium –" '

'Galactic angels – like puppies in the empyrean! If you're going to poke fun –'

'I can't read your writing. Read it to me, please.'

'Here?' I snatched back my notebook.

'You're trying on people's writing styles like trying on their clothes.'

'I'm studying great authors to develop my own style. It will incorporate the best of them all.'

He looked into his remaining sandwich and finding it empty of meat frowned his three-tuck frown.

I said, 'Perhaps you can identify this:

'Love and Death reap the desert wastes, the dark millennia of time and space are ablaze with glory. When Death dies, Love triumphs, the cries of man and beast mingle with the

48

hum of the universe. Nothing is lost, nothing is past. Maurice kneels on the pavement among the empty cartons, the castaways which yesterday were sought, bought and paid for. He suffers from a sense of loss, yet the sickly sweet taste of success clings to his tongue like fur.'

I paused. He shook his head. 'That was from a Booker winner. I've sharpened it up but it doesn't really appeal to me. Here's something from the classics:

'When I had retired to my chamber I reviewed the events of the day, meditated on the circumstances attending our first encounter. Such chilly hauteur on his part and proper modesty (I trust) on mine. I recalled how the lofty scowl on his otherwise handsome features had melted to manly frankness, freeing me from the constraint I had been obliged to maintain in his presence. Reader, picture if you will the sweet imaginings which visited me that night, the dreams attending my pillow, only to be rudely snatched away by the sound of I knew not what. Followed by a burst of fiendish laughter and the crash of breaking glass. I sprang out of bed. The night was intensely dark and still, the echo of that demon laugh hung in the air. I flung a robe about me and opened the door of my chamber. In the dim-lit corridor I beheld a shape, scarce animal, still less human –'

'Maurice?'

'If you don't approve of what I'm doing, do you know a better way?'

'Miss Zeph, it seems to me if you want to be like nobody else you've got to look inside yourself. Like breathing, no one else can do it for you.'

I gave him a look, what my mother calls one of mine, as if I have them ready-wrapped to hand round, gathered up my notebook and went.

But I was due for another of life's lessons, the one about you're never so low that you can't be shoved lower.

There was a panda car outside our house, a policeman at the wheel, a policewoman beside him. As I opened our gate she called, 'Miss Pollock?'

'Yes.'

She got out of the car, took me by the elbow. 'Zephrine Pollock?'

'Am I under arrest?'

'May we go into the house?' She was a head taller than me, her blonde hair done up in a knot, her hat perched on top and tipped over her eyes. She had one of those dot-and-carry hatbands. 'I need to talk to you, Zephrine.'

She had come over warm, I was close enough to see little beads on her upper lip. I said, 'I haven't done anything.'

'Of course you haven't.'

I thought this was how the Jews must have felt when the Gestapo came for them. 'Why can't you talk here?'

'What I have to say shouldn't be said on the doorstep.'

'Is it because of Cousin Gladys?' She stared at me, she was wearing blue eye-shadow. I said, 'I don't know anything about any of that.'

'Let's go in, shall we?'

It wasn't a request, it was an order. I opened the door. 'I'd better tell my mother you're here.'

She followed me into the hall, closed the door behind us. 'Can we sit down?'

'If you're tired.'

'There's something I have to tell you.'

She put her arm round me. Startled, I backed away. 'Look, whatever my mother's told you is only what she's been told by crazy old Gladys. My mother happens to believe it, I don't. Anyway, it's not an indictable offence.'

'Zephrine, you must be brave.'

That too was an order. Some sort of time had come because she frog-marched me into our kitchen. Of course my mother wasn't there, we'd have heard from her if she had been. The kitchen was tidy, as always, and there was the usual nice lemony smell of washing-up liquid. I remembered it afterwards, it's the sort of detail that attends moments of emotional stress.

The policewoman pushed me gently but firmly into a chair. Then she sat down facing me and tapped on the table. She was nervous, NB I thought, police have nerves.

'My name's Dawn. Not as pretty a name as yours.'

'Is this your first assignment?'

50

'What?'

I bet it was Tennyson wrote about dawn being rosy-fingered. She had big white hands that could do traffic-duty without gloves.

'Is this the first time you've nicked anybody?'

'I'm afraid . . . your mother –'

'Aren't you supposed to be a judge of character in your job? Don't listen to my mother, go and talk to Cousin Gladys. She's making a mountain out of a dog-hill.'

I smiled, but she bowed her head. 'I'm afraid there's been an accident.'

That's when I knew. Quick as a flash, quicker, I thought the unthinkable. It comes of being sensitive about words, if she'd said 'Your mother's had an accident' I'd have thought she'd just broken a leg. The de-personalizing, the 'there's been' told me in those few words.

Another thing I think of when I think of that moment is WPC Dawn's hat, that and the smell of washing-up liquid. She kept her head down and the checker pattern was all I had to look at.

'It happened so quickly, she couldn't have suffered.'

'What happened?'

'She was running to catch a bus, she tripped and fell and struck her head on a litter-bin.'

'A litter-bin!'

'She was dead before the ambulance arrived.' WPC Dawn lifted her head and looked at me, her eyelids dribbled blue. 'She couldn't have known.'

I knew. It would be one of those concrete things with the inscription 'Your borough is a garden, keep it beautiful'. 'What number bus was she running to catch?'

'Does that matter?'

'Everything matters.'

'An 84.'

'84s don't go to any place she'd be going.'

'There were eye-witnesses.'

'She wouldn't be running for an 84!' I shouted. If that was untrue all the rest must be.

'Is there someone we could contact? Your father?'

'No!'

'No relations, no aunt or uncle? Brothers or sisters?'

'No!'

'You mentioned a cousin – Gladys?'

'There's no one!'

'Zephrine, how old are you?'

'What's that got to do with it?'

'If you're alone in the world –'

'I always have been, I always will be. I'm older than I look. When I'm really old and want to look young it'll be an advantage.'

Her face had become mushy. It's what is meant by dissolving into tears. If anyone was going to do that it should be me. With nerves like hers she shouldn't be in the police.

I said, 'I'll make you a cup of tea,' and left her blowing her nose into her walkie-talkie.


I worked it out. The 84 goes across the Common and turns back at the Crematorium. We didn't know anyone on the Common or in the Crematorium.

She is buried in a churchyard under a white marble headstone and green marble chips. The chips discourage worms, the rain washes them and they sparkle. Her name sparkles: 'Mavis Pollock' and the dates of her birth and death. Nothing else. Not 'Rest in Peace', which my father wanted. I wouldn't agree to it, it would have been like putting 'Down, Rover' on her grave. I said she wouldn't be told what to do, she'd rest if she liked and if she didn't like she'd come back and haunt us. I shouted at him, and he said he'd leave it to me. She had wanted to see them together, him and Maria, doing what they did, what she imagined they did. She was my mother and I didn't like it much, but I have gone into it. I never put red flowers on her grave, red's the colour of passion, I hope she's past all that.

The way it happened is this: she believed she would have known him anywhere, although he was growing a beard it didn't make him look like George the Fifth. 'No one could be less kingly than your father.' She reserved 'Edgar' for her private use. He was still her husband and that was enough to be going on with. She was, she always had been, going on with it. I suppose she married him for the usual reasons, people seem to have them. If she didn't know what to expect she expected to like what came.

When she caught sight of him, beard and all, on the other side of the street, she was not deceived by the way he was dressed. Who but a veriest manual worker would be wearing a bomber jacket so old it must have flown every mission in World War II? She thought perhaps he was now a manual worker, perhaps that was what he had come to. And she saw that his trousers were stained yellow from painting the front gate. Their gate. Leading into the Garden of Eden, and a coal-black Eve in a grass skirt.

She would have known him anywhere. How absurd of him to think he could hide from her under old clothes and a hairy chin. From her, his wife. No man had put them asunder and no Creature could. She had known there was another side to him. She couldn't call it evil or depraved because he never went all the way with anything. She called it grubby, remembering where his formative years were formed.

So she followed him, taking pleasure in his seediness because it was what he had come to without her. She had tried to take him out of himself, it had been something she had thought she could do. She had never stopped trying, even though she wasn't getting under his skin, or if she was, he would never let her know it. At least she had kept him level with the next man.

He began running for a bus drawing into the kerb. He was too plump, he pushed the air aside with prissy movements of his hands. She thought she saw a bald patch on his crown. She was looking at it as she ran, tripped, and was struck by a stone fist between the eyes.

I told them, 'She could have been running for that bus because of someone on it, someone she thought she recognized.'

'It's possible.'

'You, for instance,' I said to him.

'Honey, he was nowhere near town.'

'Why should she run after me?'

'That's what I'd like to know.'

'To the best of my knowledge and belief I was never on an 84 bus.' When he tried to take my hand I folded my arms. 'What good can it do now?'

'Don't burden your mind, honey,' said Maria.

53

He talks about good, not doing any. Good's a gas word, it *looks* empty.

She left me the house which she had inherited. One of the things she had against him was that he had not provided her with another. She would have liked an over-provider.

' "I give and bequeath the freehold land and house, Deep-dene, and contents . . ." '

While the will was being read I was thinking that solicitors ought to be thin and dry like water-biscuits, but this one was fat and greasy.

' ". . . to my daughter, Zephrine Pollock . . ." '

His desk had a green leather inlay and a cut-glass tray full of old-fashioned pens with rusty nibs. He was using a ball-point.

'A simple testament, you are the sole legatee. I know the area, it boasts some pleasant properties. You are a fortunate young lady. Quite.' His lips made a rosebud of the word. 'Of course bereavement . . .' Broaching the subject was sufficient, he didn't have to pursue it.

People said to me 'You must be brave' or 'You're being brave', but what I should have been was something definite. Angry would have done. That's what I felt when I heard how she'd died, but it didn't last.

I wasn't shocked, or numb. My mother was killed by a litter-bin and I knew I was missing a whole gamut of emotion which as a writer I couldn't afford to miss.

' "Give and bequeath" is not her style,' I said. 'She wouldn't write that.'

'Your mother's will is perfectly valid. It was drafted in accordance with her wishes, attested and signed in this office.'

' "Give" would be enough, "bequeath" would have been better. But if you use both you weaken the sense.'

'The wording of legal documents has to be precise. Loopholes can be exploited.'

' "Hereinafter", "aforesaid", "hereinbefore" – I never heard her say that.'

Pink rose into his collar. He had a neck which registered his barometric pressure. 'We must not argue about legal terminology.'

'Crapology.'

'Miss Pollock,' he was cool, had dropped a good twenty degrees, 'you are a little overwrought. I quite understand.'

'I'm *under*-wrought.' I would like to have gone into it, just to let someone know how it was with me.

He put out a hand to his desk diary. 'Bereavement is a great leveller. You must excuse me, I have an appointment.'

My father came to the funeral service, so did Maria. They sat in the back row of the church and left before the coffin did. There weren't many mourners: Mrs Spilsbury, Cousin Gladys, a few neighbours, and two women who said they were friends but I hadn't known of them.

Cousin Gladys said that Maria coming was in the worst possible taste. She blamed him, but I think Maria had insisted on coming because she couldn't bear to be kept out of anything of his.

Four of the mourners came home with me afterwards, Gladys and Mrs S. and the two unknown women. One of them followed me into the kitchen when I went to make tea.

'I hope you like sausage rolls,' I said to her. 'They're party rolls, there weren't any funeral ones.'

'You're being very brave.'

When I took in the tea Mrs Spilsbury and Gladys were talking knee to knee and the other unknown woman was listening and had forgotten to look mournful.

I heard Mrs S. say, 'Of course she always thought he'd come back to her. She lived for the day. I used to wonder what she would do with him if it came.'

Gladys said, 'She'd have sent him away again. There would have been satisfaction for her in that, she had precious little from him otherwise.'

'She always said, "He'll come back like a dog that's been chasing a bitch." '

She wouldn't say it, it's pure Spilsbury, but it came as a surprise, welcome on the whole because it made more of a whole of Mrs S.

'She knew where he'd been,' said Gladys, 'she wouldn't have touched him with tongs.'

'Perhaps she thought the experience would have improved his technique.'

55

I realized that I had to see it from Mrs Spilsbury's angle, and from her depths, which went way down past the satin night-dress and the pompadour doll. I banged the tea-tray down in front of her.

She looked at me from both sides of her tomahawk nose and said, 'Shall I be mother?'

My father took it for granted that I was going to sell the house. 'We must find a good agent.'

Maria grinned. 'They'll put up a board says you're for sale and you'll feel you're included with the fixtures.'

'It should be an established firm, one familiar with the district.'

'That house will fetch a lot of money.'

'We must settle on an asking price. Then we can decide on a dropping price below which any offer would be unacceptable.'

'I'm not going to sell,' I said. He flinched. He isn't a planner and it was costing him to try to plan for me. 'I'm going to live in it and be happy ever after.'

'You can't. You couldn't afford the upkeep, apart from anything else.'

'What else is there?'

'You can't live in that house all alone.'

People think being alone is dire. It's basic and necessary. But it's probably only a temporary privilege. I now know about and accept the Big Bang, though I think it more of a Big Melt with so many gummy strings attaching to everyone. We'll all be back together, congealed, in the end.

Maria cried, 'We'll come and live with you!' Her joy was unconfined, she opened her arms and let it free.

'I intend to take paying guests.'

'Your daddy and me will be your guests, keep you company, pay you rent –'

'No.' He took the word out of my mouth, for which I was grateful because I didn't know how I was going to back it up.

Maria turned on him. 'Why not?'

'I can't live there.'

'It will be different, we'll be happy, the three of us will be a nice happy family.'

'No!'

Maria's face crumpled, I thought she was about to cry. She couldn't see that her idea of a happy family would disjoint the past, virtually dismember it, just when the past was tied up ready to put away.

He didn't even want to come to the house. I said he must because something of his was still there, a tin trunk full of his clothes. He said he didn't want them. Maria said he should at least look, he could do with a winter coat and woollen vests.

'I can do without.'

'She kept them for you,' I said. 'She wanted you to have them. You shouldn't snub the dead.'

'She tended them for you,' said Maria. 'I'll go, I'll fetch them.'

'She always said he was to open the trunk. She didn't know she was going to die, but she thought she might be out when he called and she made me promise never to let anyone else touch it.'

He came in the end, Maria insisted. She bounced in as soon as I opened the door. He stood waiting to be asked, he had something to get over besides the doorstep.

Maria couldn't wait. She seized his hand and pulled him in, my mother's enemy dragged my father into the house where my mother had waited for him, cherishing the clothes he had left behind. There are things you can't reconcile because they're someone else's joke. This one was at my mother's expense. Just when I had thought the dead were immune.

Maria, on her toes, spinning, was taking in and pointing out as if my father and I were the ones who had never seen the house before.

'It's nice, a nice old house, look at that parky floor, and the coloured glass making wine gums on the wall. Did you ever see a bigger castor-oil bush?'

'It's a Leopard Lily.'

'You're never going to turn this nice place into a common lodging house?'

'Not common. I shall only take writers, it's going to be a writers' house.'

'Writers? What writers?'

'New ones will be welcome but I shan't rule out the older

ones. All I ask is that they're meaningful, I want meaningful people round me.'

'Hop-heads and kinkies mean the most and the woods are full of them.'

'Where's the trunk?' He was here as an act of courtesy, his last to her, in recognition of her last act of love to him. I know a theme when it turns up.

'In the attic.' I told Maria she had better wait in the hall.

'I want to see upstairs, it's not every day I see a nice house like this.'

'Let her come.'

'I bet your momma never slept in no attic.'

'Of course not.'

'So which was her room? Can I see inside?'

'No.'

'Why not?'

'Surely you don't have to ask that?'

She looked at my father, her mouth squared like a pillar-box. He turned and went up the stairs.

'The trunk's in there,' I said when we got to the attic. 'Just as she left it.'

'Did you never look inside?' said Maria.

'Certainly not. It's between them. And he'd prefer to be on his own when he opens it.'

She pushed past me, took and held his arm, looked up at him, asking. If I had feelings like that I wouldn't let other people see them.

I waited on the landing. It was, or should have been, between him and my mother. She might have left a message in the trunk. If she had, I hoped he would keep it to himself.

Through the open door I saw him unlock the trunk and throw back the lid. Maria reached inside. She seemed to be stirring and delving.

Then she started throwing things into the air as if she was throwing confetti at a wedding. My father turned, passed me and went downstairs without a glance.

Maria held out her fist. When she opened her fingers things jumped in her palm. A square of silk fell to the floor.

58

I went and looked in the trunk. It was full of little squares, bright, dark, thick, thin – squares of cloth. Of clothes. Everything he had worn, coats, shirts, ties, trousers, pyjamas, socks, his check-patterned dressing-gown – the checks halved, quartered, diced – everything cut to pieces.

Maria plunged her arms in to the elbows, brought up handfuls. I swear each square measured an inch exactly, no more, no less. It must have taken hours to do.

'I'll send someone round for it.'

'What will you do with it?'

'Make me a rag rug.'


I have never understood why serious writers allow their books to be classed as novels. Novel spells pulp-fiction, love stories, hospital romances. Any book of mine will be novel in the best sense, new and strange, teleologic, which means interpretation in terms of purpose. I found it in the dictionary and it covers everything.

I am ready to begin a blaze of ninety thousand words. It will take a lot of thought and time, and if my writing-time is to be limited to what I can snatch after work and at weekends, all the other time will pile up uselessly. I don't intend to let it happen.

I wrote to the Hogarth Press, the publishers of Virginia Woolf. Theirs is the quality imprint I want. I got a letter from people called Chatto and Windus, suggesting I send a sample of my work of not more than two thousand words, with a synopsis of the rest. I rang them up and said I'd rather come and discuss the matter.

'Matter?'

'Of my work – you publishing it.'

'I'm afraid I didn't quite catch your name.'

'Zephrine Pollock. I'm not just writing any old hackneyed novel, you know. I'm breaking with literary conventions. As publishers of the first edition of my book you'll have the copyright of a new narrative system. Of course there'll be plagiarists, imitation is the sincerest form of envy –'

'Miss Pollock, we would be interested to see something of your work. If you care to send –'

'I'm not prepared to disclose my method at this stage.'

'I'm afraid we can't discuss your work without sight of it.'

'If you're afraid,' I said, 'let me talk to Mr Windus.'

'I'm afraid that's not possible –'

'What about Mr Chatto?'

'Any sample of your work you care to send will be carefully considered by our readers. We do ask that you enclose a stamped addressed envelope for its return.'

I know an Establishment Voice when I hear it, this one was red brick. 'I bet you didn't ask Virginia to send a stamped addressed envelope.' I rang off.


You're supposed to go to the churchyard to think about your loved one and sort yourself out, you're directed to do that. A notice on the gate says you're to 'heal and re-create your spirit' – ie remember but don't grieve. And don't remove the flower vases.

My memories are of her running for a bus and cutting up his clothes, neither of which I had actually seen her do. And my spirit was too fragmented for re-creation.

Her slippers are in the hall and the shopping basket she had with her. They brought that back empty, they said there'd been a bag of flour and a dozen eggs in it. The bag burst and the eggs broke when she fell. I have WPC Dawn's word for it. She was assigned to see me through the inquest and bring home my mother's clothes. Effects, she called them and tried to stop me looking through them because of the blood. She took an un-professional interest in me and invited me to her place for supper. I went for the experience.

It wasn't worth having. She lives with her parents and they live for her. They talked about 'our Dawn' as if she was their private renaissance.

'Family life is so precious,' she said. 'I'd like you to feel free to share ours.'

I didn't open the door to her after that. She telephoned several times and I pretended to be an answering machine. I made the mistake of asking who was calling before I started on the bit about leaving a message following the blips. However, she got the drift and left me alone.

I like being alone. I have things going on, furtherances which take up where memories leave off. I go into my mother's bedroom and see her making her bed, tucking in the blankets with a jabbing movement. I can tell it vexes her, anything that has to do with the bed does. When I was a child I asked, 'Why are you angry with the bed?' She wouldn't answer.

I say, 'You know that what you're feeling is only reflexive?'

'You know nothing about it.'

'That's what Maria says.'

'She knows more than you ever will.'

When I open a tin of beans – she would never have tinned beans in the house because of the smell – she says, 'Did you see his face when he opened the trunk?'

'No, but you did.'

'It was my privilege. We're allowed to tie up loose ends. Some of us would get restive otherwise.'

'How did he look?'

'He has a face like a clock. But I could see through to the software.' She laughs, she often laughs now. 'You'd be surprised how soft it is.'

'Wasn't there anyone else you could have married?'

'No one!'

Her voice is light and young. I'm glad she's happy – extraterrestrially. I haven't liked to ask what I really want to know, what she was thinking when she cut up his clothes. She might tell me in so many words, all carnal.

She didn't live in this house until after she married. I'm not to imagine her having her childhood here. I can't imagine her ever having a childhood. She says it was just like mine, we're no different she keeps saying, I'm her only flesh and blood now. I say she provided me with a body which I'm not too pleased with. My gift, I keep telling her, doesn't come from her, or from him. She says what gift and I tell her afflatus, which is generally considered to be divine. From where she is she ought to understand that.

Maria keeps pestering me to move in with them. She thinks the house is bad for me, empty rooms are bad. I tell her my rooms are full of furniture. She says chairs and tables aren't people, I can sleep on the sofa in their front room and have half their wardrobe to put my clothes. Maria likes a crush, she thinks anything over twelve inches between one person and the next is isolation.

'It's my home,' I say, 'I was born there. I couldn't work any-where else.'

'Aren't you afraid of duppies?'

'What?'

'Bad spirits. Houses keep the spirits of everybody that ever lived in them.'

'Are you saying my mother's spirit is bad?'

'We've each got a bad one. We die and leave it to work out the badness.'

I tell her she's been reading Shakespeare.

But I can't afford to be alone. I get bills for things I've used – kilowatts and therms and units and insurance, I'm told how to pay and with what sort of money – cheque, postal order, direct debit, giro.

I knew that you have to pay to get your dustbin emptied and the streets lit, but not how much it cost. My mother took care of all that.

There's no way I can maintain this house on my salary, even if I'm prepared to go on working, which I'm not. I'm going to write my book, I'll need every hour. Looking up 'Poll Tax' in Chambers I saw 'pollock' three words farther on. A pollock's a cod-fish.

My father offered to help. 'The money I've been paying her can now come to you.'

I said, 'What money?' It was him made me a pollock.

Maria answered. 'Surely you know he kept her?'

'She had a job, she kept herself.'

'He paid her. The first of every month, sure as day come, he paid. We went without, she didn't. I told him you can't buy an easy mind, it's something you got to give yourself.'

My mother let him off two hooks when she died: the husband hook and the father hook. I used to think it was me who connected them, but it was she who connected us. If he's anybody's, he's Maria's now.

I thought of changing my name, my writing-name. But why should I? It's ancestral, it's lineal. Weren't we all fishes in the beginning?

62

He said, 'The money won't solve all your problems but it will help.'

'I can solve my own problems.'

'I want you to have it –'

Maria cried, 'Listen to this generous man, going to give our living away!'

'It's all right,' I said, 'I'm not his wife, he doesn't have to keep me.'


I wrote on a postcard: 'Rooms to let. Only writers need apply.' When I took it to the corner-shop, prepared to pay for space in the window, the woman said, 'Writers? What writers?'

'People who write,' I said. 'They don't have to be published.'

'I don't take kinky ads,' she said.

I thought of calling it the Mavis Pollock Centre, but it was more of a lay-by. People came and went. They didn't like the amenities. There was only one bathroom and I don't allow anyone to use the kitchen before eight-thirty in the morning or after eight at night. I have my breakfast there at eight am and work there from eight pm for as long as it suits me.

A woman came, saying she was a writer. When I asked what she wrote, she said books. I said, 'Have you been published?'

'Hell, yes,' she said. I asked who by and she said just about everyone.

'I don't know your name, what are the titles of your books?'

'I can't remember.'

'Can't remember?' Shocked, I cried, 'You must!'

'Is it important?'

'Of course it is!'

'Okay,' she said, '*Woman's Journal.*'

I wanted to turn her away but I needed the rent so I put her in the second-best bedroom. She moved in, bringing a back-pack.

'Haven't you got any more luggage?'

'This is my all.' She pointed to the words 'Army reject' on the flap of her knapsack. 'I didn't even make the Falklands.'

I gave her a gas-ring so that she could make tea. She cooked on it. The smell of sausages when I was going up to bed disturbed me. When I complained she said, 'There's no table-dotey. You should put one on the door, what you can and can't do in places like this.'

'Places like what?'

'Digs. Roomers.'

'A table d'hôte is a menu for meals.'

'Isn't that what we're talking about?'

She was muscular and had a blue jaw. Finding a cut-throat razor in the bathroom I wondered if she was a man in drag. She was quiet in an officious way, crept about and made the floorboards creak, shushed herself in the hall, then climbed the stairs panting like a Dobermann. She played her radio late at night with the volume turned down. I had the room next to her and couldn't make out whether it was voices or music she was listening to. It was worse than either.

I asked when she did her writing. She said she was thinking. I said so was I and wasn't it a strain. She agreed. 'Hell, yes, you can say that again.'

I was so inexperienced as a landlady I hadn't asked for rent in advance. At the end of the first week she said she wouldn't be paid until the end of the month, then there would be a big cheque.

'Royalties?'

She nodded and drew breath as if I'd touched a vital spot. She went the night before the last day of the month. It was one time she didn't make the boards creak, I heard nothing.

After that I had a man who was writing a seed catalogue. He said the state of the market required beautiful words to go with the pictures, what he was doing was more than a sales brochure, it was a composition. He needed absolute peace and serenity while he was giving his mind to flowers and colours and scents and biodegraded composts. He gave a lot of his mind in the bathroom which he said was the most peaceful room in the house. I mentioned that the pipes hooted when the cold tap was turned on and he said he never used cold water. I was glad when he left to take up a job as cactus and succulents adviser in the Midlands.

Two girls came, one golden-haired and giggly, the other dyed orange and black-browed. She was what people call striking.

She claimed to be a published poet and showed me a paperback on recycled cardboard.

I opened it. The poems were very short. I couldn't think what to say about them, so I said, 'They're very short,' and she said, 'They're all in four-letter words.'

I asked the other girl what she wrote.

'She's my inspiration,' said Orange. 'We want a room with a double bed.'

There was only my mother's room. I cleared out her things from the wardrobe, dressing-table and chest of drawers, took away photographs and a picture called 'Betrothed' of a man and woman embracing. The girls said their names were Marks and Spencer, Mrs Marks and Miss Spencer. I thought of them as Giggly and Orange.

I invited them to have supper with me the evening they moved in. 'Tell me about your work.'

'She's a hairdresser, I type,' said Orange.

'I meant your poetry. Don't you find four-letter words restricting?'

'That's the idea, restriction. When I'm through with them I'll go on to five.'

'I suppose it does give you a format.'

'This a moussaka?' Giggly sounded incredulous.

'My idea is to make a writers' house here, a centre where writers can live together and discuss their problems with each other.'

'Good notion,' said Giggly. Orange cleared her plate. Giggly poured the last of the Lambrusco rosé, which had something in it like the foetus of a tadpole.

'Very nice, whatever it was,' said Orange. Giggly drank the wine and the tadpole.

'I'm writing a book about Napoleon.' It had come to me a split second before, out of the blue, no ascertainable cause. It was inspiration, of course, but I did wonder why Napoleon. He lost Waterloo and was banished to an island and I have never thought much more about him. Yet this was the message I'd been waiting for – it's how inspiration works. I knew what I was going to write.

Giggly and Orange quarrelled irrevocably soon after. Giggly walked out. Orange stayed. She was secretive and took to jogging round and round the garden.

One day she came in saying there was a totter outside.

'A what?'

'Asking for you.'

It was Montrose, in a country-and-western suit, white, with fringes. On his chest a gold chain, on his head a broad-brimmed straw hat. He held the push-bar of a pram.

'Is there a baby in that?' I said.

'It's transport for your father's box. I'm to take it to him.'

'He doesn't want it.'

'Maria does.'

'It's not her box. My mother left it to my father.'

'I'm told his clothes are in it.'

'What's in the box is between my parents, no business of Maria's. Or anyone else's.'

'I don't mind what's in it. If you don't wish to part with it, okay.'

He raised his hat and was turning away. I said, 'Come in and have a cup of tea.'

'Thank you. I must first put the brake on.'

Wedging a stone under the wheel of the pram, he said, 'Maria believes if you chop up a man's clothes, you chop up the man.'

We had tea in the kitchen. The kitchen is my preferred place, everything is to hand – food, gas, water, pots and pans. If I'm obliged to move around when I'm writing it breaks my train of thought.

I drink my tea, Montrose takes his. He raised the cup in slim brown fingers fanned, but not crooked, sipped with pursed lips, I didn't see him swallow. His ears moved slightly, that was all. I could see a baked bean on the table, one bean in tomato sauce, just where he might put his elbow.

'How's the writing going?'

'I have begun my book.'

'Are you pleased with what you've done?'

Pleased is the wrong word, what I feel goes a lot deeper. Call it awe, vision, superception. Call it fright.

'Is this where you work?' He was observing my notebooks and my Chelsea Bond Cream Wove A4 typing paper. There are exactly five hundred sheets, I have opened the block and checked. For ninety-thousand words at three hundred and sixty

66

words to a sheet, ten chapters of nine thousand words, twenty-five sheets to each chapter, top and one carbon, I'll need more. My first book will be written on this kitchen table. People like a humble beginning. My other magna opera will be penned at a desk with a leather inlay, looking out at a wall, some old pink wall glowing in the sun. A view would distract me. I shan't be using a word processor, it's too mechanized.

'May I read it?'

'I don't let anyone read my books until they're finished.'

'That's right.'

'It's about Napoleon. The inner man. I'm not concerned with events.'

'They must come into it.'

'Only as they affected him. Like the weather. St Helena's the tip of a volcano, it gets a lot of bad weather.' I worried he would put his country-and-western elbow on the baked bean. 'You can take the trunk.'

'You've been doing research?'

'I'm not concerned with wars and politics. I'll get the dates right of course, but I'll be concentrating on the man, his life from within, his secret thoughts and dreams, what he didn't do and wishes he had.'

'How will you know?'

'It will be fictional history. History *is* fiction.'

'I should like to talk to you about that sometime. When do you expect to finish this book?'

'Writing every day, morning, noon and half the night – not just evenings and weekends, I could finish in two months, three at the outside. Outside my gainful employment that is.'

'If you give up your job how will you keep yourself and this house?'

'I'll rent out rooms.'

'Is that a good idea?'

'Do you know a better?'

'Miss Zeph, you're alone here, a young girl going to allow strangers into your home. If they do strange things, bad things, how are you going to stop them?'

'I shall only take writers, this will be a writers' house.'

I distinctly heard my mother laugh. Wherever she is, she is

able to laugh. She doesn't use her position to put me right, she just gets fun out of it.

Montrose stood up and picked the bean off his sleeve but did not embarrass me by trying to wipe off the tomato sauce. 'Shall we go find the box?'

Next time I went to Sydenham I asked Maria what he read.

'Papers, same as everyone.'

'Has he got a lot of books?'

'You want to see?'

'I'm interested to know what sort they are.'

'Go and look. He's not in.'

'I don't think I should, he wouldn't like it.'

'He's never going to know. I shan't tell him and Edgar's sleeping off his dinner. Come, I'll show you his room. It's nice, you can see the television masts at night. Edgar and me have dustbins to look at.'

It looked bare until Maria stepped over the threshold. For a small person she takes up a lot of space.

There was a narrow bed, a chair, a curtained alcove and a roll-top desk, a Greenpeace poster over the bed. The poster was interesting, about biological time, comparing the present age of the earth to that of a person of forty-six. On that reckoning the earth was forty-two when plants and trees started to grow: a year ago the dinosaurs arrived and at the weekend we had the last ice age. But we weren't here last weekend, modern man has only been around about four hours – 'like a brutish infant gloating over his meteoric rise to ascendancy'.

'Is Montrose into saving whales?'

'Not him. He's not bothered with things can't answer back. I put that poster up to cover a crack in the wall. See these bare boards? I get down on my knees and shine them.'

'Are you really going to make a rug with my father's clothes?'

'When I enjoy my painting I don't feel the cold, I could sit in the snow and paint a fire. When I don't like what I've done I'll wrap myself in his rug and be warm.'

'There aren't all that many books.'

'How many do you want? I read a book in school, I thought it was crazy stuff. The other kids said you better believe it, you can be white or you can be blue but you can't be black.'

'Blue?'

> ' "Little Boy Blue
> Come blow up your horn,
> Goat's in the meadow
> Cow's in the corn." '

'I was four years old, a little chicken-shit thing, I wanted to change my colour, I said I'd like to be blue, but the book didn't tell me how to do it.'

I had seen something called *Les Précieuses ridicules*, by Molière. I haven't got round to the French classics yet. As a title, 'Precious Sillies' didn't recommend itself.

'I've got more books than he has. He hasn't got Dickens or Hardy or Walter Scott. He hasn't even got Shakespeare.'

'Got books in his belly.'

When she went away to get tea I took down the Molière. I was hoping for a clue to what might be silly and precious to Montrose. The book was one of those antique jobs, leather-bound, with marbled pages and a clasp. The clasp had a key-hole and was locked. So that's it, I thought, opening my mind. I'm never sure whether a darker side is weakness or strength, but if it's French, subtle and pornish, it's Art.

'No one told me you were here.'

Edgar, my father, standing in the doorway had his mystified look, his hair on end, he was collarless. He is not a commanding man, yet he commanded extremes of feeling in my mother and in Maria.

I put the precious sillies back on the shelf. Even a locked book tells you something: viz it's locked because it's frank. Explicit. Call it what you like, or don't like, sex has more words to its name than anything else I can think of – suspect words, dragooned words, perverted words. I'll make a list some day.

'I was asleep. I happened to see your coat in the hall. Why didn't Maria waken me?' He was fretful, being able to keep your temper ought to be a strength, but suppose you never had one to lose? 'What are you doing up here?'

'Looking at Montrose's books.'

69

'You come so seldom.'

'I don't have time for visiting. I'm working all day, remember. And there's the house. When I have a full complement of writers I'll give up my job and concentrate on my book.'

'You could do that now. You could sell the house, live on the money, live here with us.'

'There's no room. I need privacy and peace.'

'You could have this room.'

'It's Montrose's room.'

'He could move out, he talks of getting a place to himself.'

'I'm going to stay on in our house.'

'If it's because of Maria, we could take a flat, just you and me.'

'Maria? Of course it's not, it's because I'm going to make the house a centre for creative writers.'

'I'd give you a regular allowance, you could write all day, I'd never interfere, I'd provide for both of us.'

'You couldn't leave Maria.'

He shook his head. 'We'd be happy on our own.' I could see he believed that, had been nursing it. For how long? Perhaps all along. If someone seriously wants something of you and you know there's no way you're going to give it, you panic.

'I don't want to live with you!' It came out as a small shout. I was scared of being over-ruled. To the best of my knowledge he has never over-ruled anyone, but I sensed I was up against something entrenched. 'It's not personal,' I said.

It was, but the reasons concerned me, not him.


Chapters one and two will be transitional/traditional, phasing from conventional narrative to a system of dazzling simplicity, unambiguous and positive, at once clear to the meanest intelligence and exalting to the highest. But I'm having trouble getting started.

Orange was in the kitchen using the toaster. I asked her how she started.

'I've got a repeater alarm that wakes me after the fourth attempt.'

'On your poetry, I mean. How do you start a poem?'

'I don't think about it. My sodding toast's burnt.'

'I can't stop thinking –'

'This thing's faulty.'

'It's the setting – Harvest Brown. I like my bread well done.'

'Poetry's like bowel movements, if you think about it you can't do it. You just have to let it come.'

She chanted:

> 'Reap the mild morn
> Ride the wild noon
> Live the dead hour
> Sing a gay tune.
> To your self be kind,
> Keep your cool mind
> Hide the part which none must find.
> Take no love, no wife, take time
> And long, long, long sing your gay song,'

and threw the toast into the pedal-bin.

Naturally, I was impressed. Without stopping to think, off the top of her head – a head brimming with poetic licences – she could create an entire ode or sonnet or whatever. I was in a chronic state of underachievement and my confidence rocketed to zero. Rockets can go down as well as up.

Then I had a thought that although it did just come, it was not necessarily at this minute just past, not on the spur. She could be reciting something she wrote days ago, worked and agonized over just as I have to. This could be an elegy for her dear departed. For Giggly.

'I'm sorry about Miss Spencer,' I said.

'Who?'

'Your inspiration.' We might have that in common, her losing hers and me not finding mine.

'Is there a good reason why I shouldn't have a toaster in my room?'

'I don't allow cooking upstairs.'

'Toasting's not cooking.'

'It's a culinary operation.'

'I've always cooked in bedsits.'

71

'I think you'll find the agreement was for the rent of the room and use of cooking facilities.'

'Where will I find the agreement?'

'I told you you could use the kitchen.'

'It was verbal.'

'You agreed on a rent of sixty pounds a week for a double room, use of bathroom and cooking by arrangement.'

'There were two of us then.'

'The rent's for the room, not the people.'

'I don't need the room. I need something smaller. A lot smaller. Give me a cupboard, I want to be cribbed, cabined and confined.'

'Perhaps Miss Spencer will come back.' I meant to be comforting, but she laughed, the first time I had heard her laugh. Giggly used to do it for them both, she did it too often, but I'd rather have heard her. 'There's the attic,' I said, 'the ceiling slopes and you have to walk on your knees.'

'I'll take it for twenty a week.'

'I'm sorry, I couldn't –'

'Twenty-five and a toaster. That's my final offer.'

I cleared the attic with bad grace: with better grace I'd have dug the spiders out from the corners, but it wasn't a cost-effective operation, it was more work for less money.

My finances harassed me. The small legacy my mother had left was dwindling fast. Orange's rent supplied a fraction of the general out-goings. My salary was a long way short of supplying the rest.

I applied to the bank for a loan and was asked what I could offer as collateral. I said, 'My expectations.' Eyebrows were raised. 'I expect paying guests and an advance on my book.'

'You have written a book?'

'About Napoleon.'

'Ah, history. It has been commissioned?'

'I don't write to order.'

The eyebrows knotted, then untied. 'Have you considered taking out a mortgage?'

'Have you considered what "mortgage" means? Dead pledge.'

A girl brought the eyebrows tea but didn't offer me any.

Then I had a letter from Nell saying she was coming home, she and Boris and someone called 'Diggy'. She said she was yearning to see me.

I was totally unprepared to have them arrive on the doorstep in pouring rain two nights later. Nell flung her arms round my neck before I even realized who she was. I stepped back, caught my heel on the mat and we finished in a heap on the floor.

Nell peppered me with kisses. 'Same old Zeph! Two left feet and can't stand on either. You haven't changed – beetle brows and a bang. My, it's good to see you!'

She hadn't changed, there was some more of the same of her, more colour, more bosom, another half pound of hair piled on top of her head. I tried to close the door against the rain which was beating in, but something prevented me. It was shaped like a mushroom on a long stalk. When it moved into the light I saw that it was a man with a flat hat and a humpback, carrying two suitcases. He had his foot in the door and rain tipping off his hat.

'Give her a kiss, Boris,' said Nell. 'He's dying to meet you.'

She hadn't retained the fact that I dislike being touched. I retreated, he stepped after me and scooped me into a close relationship with whiskers as soft as a wet kitten. I got another shock when a face looked into mine from the hump on his back. Nell was saying they'd been travelling for days and were ready to drop right here on the step and I was discovering that the hump wasn't a hump but a papoose, a child carried Indian-fashion in a sort of wicker funnel.

'We came via Yosemite National Park, so Boris could see the rocks.'

I knew what was going to happen: you know Nell Peppiatt for five minutes and you see your future unfolding. I said to myself, this is my house, I decide who's to live in it. To Nell I said, 'This is a centre for creative artists.'

'Boris is a creative artist.'

'Writers – people I can talk to about writing.'

'You can talk to me.'

'Nell, I'm sorry – but I need the money.'

'We'll pay, we'll pay whatever you ask.'

'I don't know what to ask you.'

'The same as you'd ask Kingsley Amis and Beryl Bainbridge.'

'I must have the rooms ready to show people.'

'We only want one room.'

'I couldn't make a reduction for you being you, I'd have to charge the full amount.'

'Mrs Trompetto let us off the rent while Boris was doing her horse. He could have got two thousand dollars for it in New York. She was getting the equivalent of two-hundred and fifty for a top back-room and a tub in the closet.'

'I couldn't let you have the room for less than eighty pounds a week sharing the bathroom and kitchen. And cooking facilities aren't available after eight pm.'

I hoped to discourage her, but she said, 'Boris does the cooking. We'll tide you over until some writers turn up.'

The papoose was their child, a shrimpish creature with a hook nose. 'He's got a hook nose,' I said.

'Like his father. Zeph, it's great that you haven't changed. I loved you as you were and I still do. I wouldn't have you internally different. But your hair does nothing for you, I've seen horses' tails with more style.'

'Boris hasn't a hook nose.'

His is cleft at the tip, more of a knuckle-bone. He is over-extended, when he gets excited he shoots out of his clothes, adds inches to his stature. It would be impressive if his sleeves and trouser bottoms did not shrink to compensate. He has a mat of East European curls and eyes which slip to and fro like fish. He's homely. That isn't a fault, but it vexes me the more when Nell criticizes my appearance.

They stayed. I gave them my mother's room, the one Orange had vacated. They fitted two armchairs together for the child. 'A temporary measure,' said Nell. 'We'll get something with bars to keep him in, and when Kingsley and Beryl come we'll go.'

'There's nowhere for Boris to sculpt.'

'He'll manage.'

'He can't cut stone in the bedroom!'

'Don't worry. He's into bone sculpture. We got the idea from a commercial showing what happened to chickens after they've been eaten. The carcasses are stripped and the bones processed for the Third World, for fertilizers and pep pills. Nothing's wasted. The little bones look like three-dimensional jigsaw pieces, they pass to the mill on a conveyor belt. Boris was inspired. He makes lovely abstracts, no two the same.'

'If it means cooking –'

'The whole process is gentle and quiet, won't disturb anyone. It's a new art form and supplies the answer to our overcrowded cemeteries. By the year two thousand and eighty-four we'll be reprocessing ourselves, goodbye Everglades, maggots and funeral pyres, just sacks of nice clean powder.'

'It's a horrible idea.'

'Why shouldn't we push up beans instead of daisies?'

'I don't like it.' I actively disliked the idea of chicken bones being reassembled in my mother's bedroom.

'Zeph, if you're not buried or burned you end up a fossil.'

'Can you afford eighty pounds a week?'

'Remember that piece you did about the Lady of Shalott in her tower?'

'What's that got to do with it?'

'I never forgot it. It was good.'

'You couldn't pay your rent in America –'

'Trompetto was a philistine. Boris carved that horse and it was a wonderful centrepiece. But she said it wasn't complete, a horse standing on its back legs shows all it's got. You've fudged it, she said. I said, "Mrs T., that horse isn't an anatomic specimen, it's a work of art." It was wasted in her back-yard. Now here, on your front lawn –'

'It's understood,' I said, knowing that understanding takes two and there was no guarantee of her understanding my un-derstanding, 'that when a writer applies, you'll vacate the room?'

'Who are these people?' Maria said.

'Nell's a friend from schooldays.'

'I remember what she did to you,' said my father.

'That was just a bit of fun, she was trying to make me look glamorous. In the absence of a writer to occupy the room, there's no one else I would wish to have it. She's my oldest friend and she believes in me.'

75

Montrose said, 'Will she help you with your writing?'

'My writing's inner-motivated, but she'll give me practical support. I need her belief.'

'What about his?' cried Maria. 'Your own father's?'

'I gave up my ownership of him when he gave up his of me.'

It was an exit line, I exited on it. But Montrose came after me. 'I've been meaning to ask, why do you choose to write about Napoleon?'

'I didn't choose, I was inspired. I only ever thought about him in school and when I passed the Empress Josephine, that's the pub on the corner of Waterloo Terrace. More often I thought of the railway station and going to the seaside with my mother.'

'Maria doesn't know how your mother felt, she thinks it's how she feels herself. Jealousy doesn't come easier the second time round.'

'What does she see in him? Do you think it's the same as my mother saw?'

'A black girl's not obliged to love only a black man.'

'I intend to use Napoleon as my blueprint for humanity which is what creative fiction is all about. My opening chapter is a straight plunge into the narrative: "He stood in the prow, watching through the swirling mist as the island approached, his last landfall, his last prison. Or was it to be the gate to freedom, to ever more glorious triumphs? To world domination!" There'll be some general philosophy, an in-depth description of the he- and she-cabbage trees that grow on St Helena, I think of bringing them in as symbolic of the departure from single-cell evolution, the birth of sex. Of humanity.'

'Going to be a great book, Miss Zeph.'

'Please don't call me "Miss", it's straight out of *Uncle Tom's Cabin*.'

Diggory means 'an exposed child'. And a hero of romance, according to my dictionary. He'll never be that.

Released from the papoose pack he proved to be very small, an undersized child more than a baby. He has a condensed yellowish face and a hook nose. His eyes are suspicious. He's very active, gets all over the house at speed, one leg grabbing and the other doubled under him. I asked Nell how old he was.

'Why?'

'Because he's too old. It's only months since you wrote saying you were expecting him.'

'He's very advanced. Nowadays kids switch to fast forward in the womb.'

He doesn't like me, he uses his dormant leg to kick when he can get close. Orange didn't like him. She told me to keep him out of her room. I said he couldn't get up the attic stairs, could he? She said so soon as her back was turned he was under her bed. I told her to lock her door. She said, every time she went to the bathroom? Every time she came down to the kitchen to boil a potato? I said I'd speak to his mother.

Nell said, 'I can't keep him chained up. He's got an enquiring mind. Like me.'

'She's the only writer I've got, I have to keep her sweet.'

'She should welcome the chance of watching a young life unfold.'

'He's not like you. Or Boris.'

'Well, it's Boris you must talk to. I shan't be around, I'm taking a job.'

'What sort of job?'

'With a packed-dinners company.'

'You know about packed dinners?'

'I picked it up in the States. Diet's one of their holy cows. And I've eaten enough meals on planes and long-distance buses to qualify as an expert. That's something you should do.'

'Eat packed dinners?'

'Travel. You're insular.'

'A writer has to be an island.'

'You have to be a continent as well. Get off your butt and go round the world.'

'What would I use for money?'

'Sell this place. You'd sell your problems with it.'

'I can handle my problems. I'm going to make this house a literary Mecca.'

'You've absolutely no business sense, you'll never make it pay.'

'Why not? If two can live as cheaply as one, four can live as cheaply as two, and six can live as cheaply as three.'

'Oh my Gud!' She says 'Gud' since she's been in America.

'But I'll never get people to stay if you don't keep Diggory out of their rooms.'

'Who could object to a tiny baby?'

'He's not a tiny baby, he must be getting on for two years old.'

She still laughs the way she always did, at me and with me, and I still feel foolish. I don't think Nell's ever felt foolish, not even that time I told her she'd picked up my father.

She said coolly, 'He's twenty-two months. I was going to tell you anyway. But you mustn't tell anyone else, especially not Boris.'

'He must know!'

'It's not the sort of thing that registers with him. Fortunately. At this point it would only complicate matters. Once, of course, it would have nipped them in the bud. Diggory's not his. He derives from a mine-sweeper I met at a time when I was under the popular illusion that giving birth would make me a whole woman.'

'A mine-sweeper!'

'It was his job. I was whole and so was Diggory by the time I met Boris.'

'What happened to the mine-sweeper?'

'He was swept up by a mine. I had to cover that episode. Where Boris comes from it's a man's sacred duty to make women whole, as many women as possible. If they turn out to have been made whole already by someone else, it's no longer sacred, or a duty, it's carnal indulgence and the man gets no points for it.

'I saw how it would be with Boris, he wouldn't accept me and he certainly wouldn't accept Diggory. So I didn't tell him. I left Diggy with my landlady and moved in with Boris and at the first plausible moment announced I was pregnant. It was really sooner than plausible because Boris was raised in ignorance of the female system. He thinks it's teamed with the lunar cycle and if you want a baby you make love when the moon's full.' Nell laughed. 'Can you credit it? If life was that simple! He was

78

bucked when I said I was expecting, happening so swiftly it confirmed his virility. I foresaw trouble in not getting big so I ate blow-up food – pasta and cereals, bread, potatoes, candy, burgers, fries, drank gallons of water and slipped myself table-spoonfuls of salt. I put on pounds, I must say I enjoyed being a pig. I was so fat Boris was sure I was carrying a superman.'

'You didn't have to lie to me.'

'I wrote that letter to convince myself. Besides, I didn't lie, I just re-timed the truth. I had Diggory one day while Boris was out. When he came home I was propped up in bed with the little stranger wrapped in swaddling clothes beside me.'

'Surely he didn't believe it was a newborn baby!'

'Anyone who believes you can sit on a stool and talk sense while you're giving birth, can believe anything. And Diggy has always been small.'

After that I was less than keen to approach Boris on the subject of keeping Diggory under control. Although Boris did their cooking and I encountered him in the kitchen, we had never actually conversed. He shouted and waved the bread-knife at me. He wore a butcher's apron and made me nervous until I realized that he was asking where things were. I tried being friendly, brought up relevant topics like the weather, gas-mark five and President Bush. Boris made a deeply involved face and went on pounding steaks. I found out later that Nell had told him I wrote in the kitchen and must not be distracted.

When I was sure she had gone out I went up to their room to make my complaint. The last thing I wanted was for her to witness the exchange. But Boris was a different man upstairs, quite the host, he asked me in and gave me a chair.

I hadn't been inside that room since they took up residence. It looked smaller, any room would with Boris in it. Also there was what they'd done to it. They'd shifted the furniture around, my mother's Lloyd Loom chairs were stacked seat to seat to make way for Diggory's cot. The double bed was over against the wardrobe and they'd hung their clothes round the walls. Nell's dresses, a cloak thing of Boris's, brushed-nylon scramble suits and a pint-size parka of Diggory's all dangled from the picture-rail. The dressing-table was spread with news-

79

paper. On the newspaper were files and picks and a little hammer. Something was boiling on the gas-ring.

'What's that cooking?'

'I am stripping my bones.'

'I don't allow cooking in the bedrooms. I told Nell.'

'It is not cooking, it is purgation. I am preparing a work of nature to become a work of art.'

'This room's too small for the three of you.' I felt pretty sick. It had never been a shrine, but it was now a squalid place, even Orange and Giggly hadn't made such a mess. The smell came from bones boiling or Diggory's smalls soaking in the hand-basin. 'Where's Diggory?'

'Gone to get candy.'

'What?'

'He is looking for someone to buy him a candy-bar.'

'It's him I want to talk to you about. He's upsetting my lodger, he goes into her room and disturbs her. She's a poet, her train of thought is fragile and easily broken.'

'I should like to talk with her. A poet!'

'She doesn't want to talk.'

'Artists must communicate with each other. Only they can understand the relation of art to life.'

I said, looking at the pot bubbling on the gas-ring, 'I can't have that. It smells awful.'

He inclined his head. 'Granted, conditions are difficult. I am not able to attempt major sculpture which is why I am working on a miniature scale. I am attempting a radically different concept of delineation. I take a natural form, already formed, already complete, limited to its natural function which is to support, contain and animate. First, I boil the bones, not too much or they will become brittle. When all the flesh has been stripped I assemble the material. I produce skeletal constructs which are works of art, the more profound for being small.'

'Please don't boil any more bones.'

'I shall make you an amulet from a furcula.'

I went upstairs looking for Diggory. Our attic landing is dark and full of noises, like Prospero's island. They're not sweet airs, they're irrigational, the water-tank has trouble with its down-pipe.

The attic room's pretty stultifying. The ceiling slopes so that you can only get out of bed on one side: the window's a stuck sash, the view is into the crotch of an oak tree. Orange had fought me over the rent. I said what did she expect for twenty-five pounds. She said living space, and I said that not having a lot of it should help concentrate her mind.

Diggory was on the floor outside her door. When stationary he adopts the fœtal position, Nell has probably trained him to. Even though I know he's not recently out of the egg, seeing him curled nose to knees, cuddling his neck, I could be deceived about his age.

I said 'Hi,' in a friendly way. 'What are you doing? Are you asleep?' Silly questions but I had to lead with something. 'It's not such a good idea to sit here, you know. Mrs Marks might fall over you when she comes out.'

There was desperation in the way he crouched against the door, as if he was trying to burrow through it. He was desperate to get into that room. What was he hoping for from Orange? A candy-bar? I don't know how deep children's passions go.

I knelt beside him. 'Come with me to the kitchen and we'll find you a chocolate biscuit.'

He butted the door with his head, his small rump stuck up defiantly. There I was – feeling it keenly – on the floor in a suppliant attitude, supplicating a troublesome child who was threatening my plans. I lost patience and pulled him away from the door.

He's undersized but not under strength. He jack-knifed, hit me on the nose and delivered a backward kick to my genitals. I yelled with pain, whereupon Orange opened her door.

'What the hell's going on?'

She had barely got the words out before that child had scuttled between her legs and under the bed. We saw his eyes glow, I could swear they were luminous.

'I'm sorry.' I struggled to my feet. 'I was trying to get him away.'

'He knocked you down?' Orange was caustic.

'He's not amenable.'

'Nor am I when I'm interrupted. Do you know how often I have to chase him out?'

81

'Why does he keep coming?'

'To annoy me. If it wasn't me it would be somebody else. Get somebody else, get more lodgers and let them have a turn.'

'What does he *do*?'

'Waits. Spiders wait, then they pounce.'

I didn't see her as a fly but it struck me that Diggory was watching from under the bed hopefully, even insistently. 'You don't encourage him? Give him sweets?'

She glared, red in the face. It looked wrong with her colour hair. When she tried to drag him out he retreated into the corner.

'Wait, I'll fetch the broom,' I said.


Although I'm the least important and the least blameworthy, I'm the most accessible in our office. I'm a sitting duck. I sit and think about my book. Mr Ginsberg accuses me of wool-gathering. Mrs Ginsberg says I'm getting intellectual.

People think it's easy to write a book, they think anyone can if they have the time, they think their time's filled with things that matter, what I call otherness. I'm keeping otherness out of my life.

I'm full of words. I shall build bridges with them when I have found what to bridge. I have no trouble now with words, it's what to make them say. I have trouble getting them to cohere. It's not enough just to throw them up, as some writers do, and leave the reader to reach for the meaning. Iris Murdoch doesn't, nor shall I.

My book's about Napoleon on St Helena, which is an ex-tinct volcano somewhere between Africa and America. I have a piece of pumice which my mother used to rub the eyes off potatoes with. If I look at it long enough I see a hard grey froth sticking out of the sea. Someone must have thought it would be a nice touch to have him sit out his days on a big chunk of pumice.

I was thinking what a nice touch it made when the phone rang on my desk. I picked up the receiver but before I could say anything a man's voice shouted, 'Who the devil's that?'

'Mr Ginsberg's secretary speaking.'

'Get off the line!'

'Can I help you?'

'Put me through to the bloody fool who wrote me about my bloody Land Rover.'

'I'm sorry, Mrs Ginsberg is not in the office at the moment.'

'I don't want to talk to a bloody woman. Put me through to Charlie Chinstrap or whatever it is he signs himself.'

'Mrs Charlotte Ginsberg wrote you about the terms of your hire-purchase agreement. I typed the letter. You must be Mr Hickson. I'll tell her you rang –'

'Don't you understand English? Who runs your bloody caper?'

'The Managing Director is unavailable at present.'

'Give me his private phone number, I'll bloody well get him at home!'

'I shouldn't be too sanguine about that,' I said.

'Listen, cookie, I'll get you – just you bloody wait!'

I rang off. There's nothing like the word 'debt' for putting people's backs up.


The porter was gone on his rounds when I left the office and went down to the lobby. A man stood in the doorway with his back to me.

'Excuse me,' I said, trying to slip past him. Then I saw my father's old trilby bending his ears. 'Oh, it's you,' I said, relieved. He said could we talk.

'Why didn't you come to the house?'

'This is between you and me.'

I think he's afraid my mother will hear him, afraid she's bugged the house, sometimes I think she's bugged the air.

'Maria has asked me to marry her.'

'You mean she's proposed?'

'It's not the first time.'

'Aren't you the lucky man.'

'I thought it was because she was pregnant.' His face looks beefy when he blushes. 'She said she was too smart to let that happen.'

'If she was really smart she'd have said she *was* pregnant.'

'I want to ask you –'

'Yes,' I said, 'I'll be bridesmaid.'

'Will you tell her why I can't marry her? She'll listen to you.'

'I don't know why you can't.'

He looked as if I'd trapped him. 'It's nothing to do with her – I've tried to get her to see that.'

'What is it to do with? I'd really like to know. I mean, it must have taken hours and hours cutting up your suits, shirts, ties, socks, hacking through your winter overcoat. But to my mother it seemed worth doing. Why?'

I saw him trying to think what to answer, and realizing that he couldn't.

He said, 'I'm more than twice Maria's age, it wouldn't be fair to tie her down. She's a free spirit.'

'Don't get metaphysical, just tell her you don't want to marry. She'll listen.'

I got a visit from her soon after that. She was white-eyed and desperate, she walked round the kitchen touching things, herself included, with spite.

'I saw a hold-all in your attic. I'd like it to put Edgar's things in.'

'What things?'

'He's going to Kingston, Jamaica. Monkey Town.' She picked up my pumice-stone.

'Be careful with that,' I said. 'It's a bit of volcano.'

She wasn't listening, she was in the lee of one of her storms. She scrubbed her fingers with the pumice until she drew blood. I can't do with temperament when I'm working.

'You can have the hold-all.'

'I can't get it back to you.'

'Are you going too?'

'You think I should walk three steps behind him, black girl, know your place?'

'I thought you loved him.' It's too gentle a word to apply to her, she wouldn't experience love, she'd explode it.

'You're his daughter but you know nothing about him. He's got trouble. Dead trouble.'

'Any trouble he has he brought on himself.'

'Trouble's trouble whoever brings it. He's got her on his back and there's no shaking her off.'

'Are you talking about my mother?'

84

'I'm talking about Dry-Bone. She'll ride with him to Jamaica. But I shan't.'

'Why not?'

Her lip, curling, quivered. 'He hasn't asked me to.'

'I'm sorry.'

'Are you sure what you're sorry for? It's because of you he's going, because you won't listen. You're his family but you turn away from him.'

'You're his family now.'

'I'm his housegirl, I wash and clean and cook for him.'

'But there's more between you –'

'You sure as hell about everything! He won't miss me on that account, housegirls thick as fleas in Port-au-Prince.' For one so flagrant she has a reserve of bitterness which I expect of secretive people.

'What will you do?'

'Burn my heart, what do you think?'

'I'll get the hold-all,' I said. 'It will be my parting present.'

Boris was the cause of Orange leaving. Boris talked, and she didn't want to be talked to.

'I was in bed working, that's where I usually work, and in he comes and sits down and tells me I'm diffusive. He kept on about the single vision and what he calls the "beautiful less". I was trapped, he was sitting on my feet.'

'He's interested in you because you're a poet.'

'When I managed to get my feet out from under him and get myself out of bed I forgot I was only wearing my pyjama top. He got the full scenario. What's with him? He can't make up his mind whether to carve fishbones or concrete.'

'Chicken bones actually.'

'He talks crap. According to him the true artist should labour to perfect one work which will live for ever. I said no one would know I was good until I was dead and I wouldn't like that.'

'He's only saying it's better to do one good thing than a lot of indifferent ones.'

'He's saying I'm not a true artist.'

'Perhaps artists ought to specialize.' I warmed to the idea. Working on one great book – a book for all time, like the Bible,

85

only modern – would concentrate my powers, crystallize my inspiration. I could afford to polish my prose and cut down my working hours.

'Go ahead, specialize,' Orange said savagely, 'but keep that weirdo away from me. If I don't get my privacy you don't get your rent.'

I appealed to Nell. She said Boris enjoyed talking to the lady upstairs. 'He gets lonely, poor old devil.'

'She doesn't.'

'Shall I go and smoothe her over?'

'Please don't! She's a poet and wants to be left alone. I don't expect you to understand, but you might at least understand that I need her rent.'

'I'm sorry things aren't going well. If I didn't have this poxy job to go to I'd be drumming up trade for you.'

What finally happened between Boris and Orange I shall never know. She told me she was deducting a fortnight's rent as compensation for harassment. The loss of working-time was irredeemable she said. What about notice I said and she said there'd been no agreement and she was going anyway. I had the feeling that I was permanently on the departure end.

Boris burst in on me crying, 'Where is the attic poet?'

'Gone.'

'Poetry has gone? Music has gone? Where is the harmony of words?' I was in for some of what Orange had endured. 'Why do you and I not communicate? We are separate entireties.'

'Entities.'

'Artists must commune through their art.'

'There'll be community when I get some writers here. We'll create our own ambience, relate to each other. But I've just lost my only paying poet because you talked too much. She had her work and she wanted to be left to get on with it. You drove her away.'

'Was she a great poet?'

'She could have been an Edith Plath or a Sylvia Sitwell, that's not the point. She's gone, and I stand to lose a hundred pounds a month.'

'Would you agree that not knowing one's limitations is as good as not having any?'

86

'I haven't thought about it.'

'It is the question which must be resolved before I can work again. I ask myself, is it a question? Is such ignorance proof of the true artist? Should I stop now? It is a question of degree.' I rolled and re-rolled the platen of my typewriter as meaningfully as I could. 'The answer is yes. I should stop. I have found my fulfilment in chicken-bones.'

He wasn't pleased about it. His eyes blazed. 'Why should I – or anyone – model in stone? There is no use for stillness, it is all motion, but no poetry. Poetry has gone.'

'She's not the only one who can write.'

'If I freeze the moment before the act, will you stop to look? There is no market for serenity. Or sublimity. Or condiments. Commercialism has degraded artistic participation. Shall Cellini make his salt-cellar when only tomato-sauce is required?'

'There's not much taste in sausages nowadays,' I said.


Then Montrose came and asked if I would take Maria in. I tried a joke, 'You mean put a tuck in her?'

'Take her into your house. It's what she wants but doesn't like to ask for fear you'll refuse.'

'I'm refusing.'

'She only wants a little place, upstairs or down, maybe an attic –'

'I'm sorry. I don't just let rooms, I'm not running a boarding-house.'

'She could help with cooking and cleaning, give you time to write.'

'She'll go to Jamaica. You'll see.'

'Edgar's already gone. You're her only link with him.'

'That's nonsense, she must have hundreds of links. It doesn't take a course in literary appreciation to know that. Why can't she stay with you?'

'It wouldn't work out.'

'It used to.'

'Since Edgar, she's not the same.'

'Well, that's not my fault.' Blame's not obligatory, you can take it or leave it. I needn't pick this one up. 'Why can't she go back to her family?'

'Aunt Luella died, there's no family without her.'

Nell was scathing when I told her Maria would be moving in. 'You're such a baby, Zeph! You're positively umbilical.'

'I'm sorry for her.'

'You let people take advantage of you.'

'Your advantage is you're my oldest friend. Maria's is that my father has done the same to her as he did to my mother and me. Anyway I like her.'

'Guess we'd better be crazy about her then.'

She happened to be sitting in the porch when Maria arrived, pushing the perambulator Montrose had fetched my father's box in. It was full of cloth bundles tied at the corners like a swagman's. Underneath, on the luggage grid, was a stack of Maria's board paintings.

Nell said, 'How clever of you to bring your things in a pram.'

'Didn't you ever see anything like it before?'

'Maria, this is Nell,' I said, 'my friend from schooldays. Nell, this is Maria Odenda.'

'Your father's friend.'

'His kept woman,' said Maria.

Nell's laugh has a cadence which can get to you. I saw it getting to Maria. I said, 'I want you to be friends.'

Diggory tried to climb into the pram. Nell caught him by the seat of his jeans and dangled him upside down.

'You're going to give that child brain damage,' said Maria.

I helped her carry her stuff upstairs. 'Why didn't he let you have the hold-all?'

'He's gone farther than me.'

Suddenly she sounded lost. In the small attic room she looked lost. Her bundles looked lost. I thought it must be how my mother looked when she was alone and knew she always would be. His talent for making women desolate simply by removing himself has psychological depths. It's material for a novelist. When I try to reconstitute that sort of relationship I'm stopped cold.

'I hope you'll be comfortable.'

'I don't want to be anywhere else, don't want to be anywhere much.'

'Forget about him. He's no good to anyone, he said so himself.'

'My good came from him.'

'Where will you put your pictures?'

'Under the bed.'

Next morning I waited around for Nell to come down. She doesn't take breakfast and she's always late getting off for work. I thought to catch her on her way out. I had something to announce, or rather to let drop.

Hearing footsteps I went into the hall, the tip of my tongue ready with oh, by the way, incidentally, did I tell you. . . . But it was Maria on the stairs.

'Good morning,' I said, 'did you sleep well?'

'With rats in the room?'

'What?'

'Big as dogs. Maybe they were dogs. I was too scared to get up and look.'

'You heard the water-tank rumbling. It does sometimes.'

'Has it got teeth?'

I started to wonder what I'd taken in besides herself. There'd been that business with Gladys and the cat's tail. 'There have never been rats here, why should they wait for you before they turn up?'

'They carried my picture away. Come and see where they left it.'

On the landing, outside Nell and Boris's door was a panel in Maria's usual style, big colours thick and glistening as if the paint was still wet. She pointed to marks along the edge. It looked as if someone had tried to eat it like a slice of bread and jam. 'Rats been chewing it.'

'Most likely it was Nell's boy, Diggory.'

'Why?'

'He's just a baby.'

'Naturally he's kinky when she carries him about like a chicken for the pot.'

'I should have told you to lock your door.'

Nell had heard us and came out on the landing, partly dressed in panty-girdle and a velvet neck-ribbon. She doesn't wear a bra. At sight of her Maria's lips got visibly smaller.

'What's going on?'

'It's Diggory again. He's savaged one of Maria's paintings.'

'He's what?'

'Chewed it.'

Nell stooped to take up the picture. No other woman with free-range breasts could do that as gracefully as her. 'What's it a picture of?'

Maria said, 'It's a fruitscape.'

'Diggory thought it was good enough to eat.'

Boris appeared, also topless, and hairy as a coconut. He looked at the picture and pronounced it a 'primitive'.

Maria bridled. 'That mean born a monkey die a monkey?'

Nell said, 'We all have the same antecedents.'

'Look,' I said, 'we should be talking about Diggory.'

Boris said, 'The true primitive is he who rediscovers our sources. The method and the medium are referrals to our way of life.'

'I paint what comes into my head.'

'You choose this rough wood to demonstrate that we live out of boxes, our houses are boxes –'

'I choose it because I can't afford anything else.' Maria snatched her picture out of Nell's hand and stamped upstairs.

'She thinks you're getting at her,' I said.

'She does not understand what she is trying to do.'

'She's trying to paint the nervous breakdown of a fruit-machine,' said Nell. 'Coloureds are more racist than anyone.'

'I expect they have to be.' I looked at my watch. 'I must go, I'm having breakfast with my publisher.' It was what I'd been waiting to let drop. And it was true enough for the time being, the time being the twenty-four hours since I had spoken to him on the telephone. Something I've learned about the book business is that it lacks vision. I've heard of best-sellers being rejected out of hand – *Watership Down* and *Pride and Prejudice* were never even read. You'd think they'd have learned from the experience of losing money, if nothing else.

I'd seen his advertisement in the personal column of our local freebie: 'Enterprising publisher seeks to extend his list. Writers with new and original material invited to apply. Submissions treated in confidence.' I liked the look of it, placed between someone seeking a companion for a walk along Hadrian's Wall, and a psychic consultant offering crystal and Tarot readings.

I rang him up. He had a smoker's cough which shattered my questions but allowed him to ask how old I was and could I use a word-processor. He arranged to see me over breakfast in the British Home Stores. I said, 'Breakfast?' and he said, 'They stop serving it at eleven.' I told him I'd have had mine by then and he said to join him for coffee.

After I rang off I realized I didn't know his name or what he looked like. Each time I rang back the line was engaged. I hoped I'd recognize him by his cough.

Quite a number of people were eating late breakfasts: bacon, sausage, egg and tomato, toast, marmalade and coffee – good value for ninety-nine pence. He was easy to locate. Discounting pensioners, men from the building-sites, mothers and babies and a girl from the Halifax, I narrowed the possibility down to two. One man was spreading marmalade on fried bread, the other was reading the *Sun*. They both looked up. The fried-bread man winked at me, the *Sun* man stared. Instinct led me to him.

He acknowledged me with a bout of coughing, a routine which opened with a wheeze, worked up to a crackling roar and exploded through a drooping Viking moustache which he mopped tenderly. It must take enterprise to grow whiskers reaching to your collarbone.

He looked me over. 'I've seen you somewhere.'

I experienced a pang which shot up through my stomach into my heart-valves. The whiskers had temporarily distracted my attention from the peppered nose above them. I said, 'It was years ago. At the Spilsburys'.'

'They had Old Tyme Dancing and we danced "Begin the Beguine".'

'We went to bed.'

'Was it a business arrangement?'

'No. You were going to show me what to do.'

'Do?'

'In bed.' I remembered the pompadour doll giving virgin birth to Mrs Spilsbury's nightdress. 'You were going to take me through the process.'

91

'I'm romantic,' he said. 'I remember my lovers, every hair, every button. I don't remember sleeping with you.'

'It was only sleeping. I dropped off. We didn't achieve anything.'

'Weren't you going to be a writer?'

'I'm writing a book about Napoleon.'

'Another *chronique scandaleuse*?'

'About his last days on St Helena.' I drew up a chair, we sat with his greasy plate and a puddle of coffee between us. I thought publishers were supposed to take you to the Ivy. 'It's about his innermost self.'

'Where are you getting the naughty bits from?'

'Are you a publisher?'

'What gave you that idea?'

'Your cough.'

'I haven't got a cough.'

'You were coughing just now –'

'I had a bit of streaky stuck in my throat.'

I looked round for the fried-bread man, but he had gone.

Maria insisted on having meals for me when I got home in the evening. She cooked in the same spirit as she paints. It comes over big in paint but shrivels food. I told her she needn't make supper, I'd get myself something.

'I know your something. You come home tired and pick an old iced-up thing out of the freezer. You got to have hot meals cooked for you, plenty of meat but no pudding, you're getting to be a banjo round the hips.'

She sat and watched while I ate. She wanted to talk about my father. I didn't, certainly not when I was chewing on leather and onions. She asked if I thought he'd been happy with her.

'Of course.'

'Every hour, every minute, Monday through Sunday?'

'Why not?'

'Because he's gone is why not and I'm thinking he wasn't happy with me any more than with your momma. Where did we go wrong?'

'Leave her out of it.'

'She was in my same shoes. I have big big feelings, what did she have?'

I nearly said she was a good cook, but then Nell came in crying 'What happened? Did you sign a contract?'

'Publishers don't draw up contracts while they're eating breakfast.'

'Breakfast?' said Maria. 'You have to sign for tea and toast?'

'Was he young, old, menopausal?'

'He's the Viking type. He's only one of several who are interested. The Hogarth Press have asked to see the first chapter of my book. I think of calling it *The Volcano*.'

'Any reason?'

'St Helena was one once. It's extinct now, of course, has been for a long time. But Napoleon wasn't, he'd have blown up the world if he hadn't been trapped among the mists and the he-and she-cabbage trees.'

'The what?'

'They're the vegetable equivalent of Adam and Eve. St Helena is the tip of a submerged mountain and the sea's all around it. The sea's where it all began, it's full of relics of the time before man, before animals, when single-cell reproduction was being superseded by sex.'

'Use your mouth to finish your steak,' Maria said.

'I'm sorry, it's awfully well done but I can't eat any more.'

'I've got antacid powders upstairs,' said Nell.

Maria bounced out, slamming the door.

'She doesn't like me.' Nell sounded plaintive. 'I'm crazy about her. So's Diggy, he follows her everywhere.'

I'd noticed, I'd seen him rowing himself up the stairs, grabbing at each tread with one leg and both arms. He kept his eyes on Maria and if she disappeared from his view he whimpered piteously. Unlike Orange, Maria waited for him. She always waited, then swept him up with welcoming cries and they crooned to each other.

'She tells him stories,' said Nell.

'What kind of stories?'

'About animals, tigers and monkeys and spiders.' Nell yawned. 'Sex or the single cell, I know which I'd choose.'

★

93

Toplady arrived with a document-case, bright blue plastic, it looked frivolous. I told myself if I signed any documents with him I'd need to watch the heretofores and whereinsoevers.

'Nice place you've got here,' he said, stepping into the hall. 'Dulwich vernacular, built for chief clerks and dentists, people who went to Bournemouth for their summer holidays. The arch over the stairs reminded them of Corfe Castle.'

He marched into the kitchen, nodded to Boris who was making beetroot soup, and went out into the garden, heading for our rose-arbour which has become an Old Man's Beard arbour.

I called, 'Where are you going?' He waved without looking round and plunged knee-deep into the undergrowth. 'You'll get wet.' Rain had been falling for hours, I could smell the vegetable kingdom.

He disappeared into the elder bushes. They shook with his passing. There are berries on them like tiny black grapes, they taste vile and stain purple at a touch.

I waited in the kitchen doorway, telling myself that this Toplady was a rogue male who was short of standards, any standards and I should expect nothing from him.

Boris said, 'Who's that?'

'A publisher.'

'What is he doing?'

'Researching into my background.'

'If there is a history in your garden it is ours, not yours.'

'How do you mean?'

'Tins. The child hides them.'

'Tins?'

'When I have done cooking – beans, tomatoes, mushrooms, olives, syrup – he hides the tins in the bushes. He is hoarding.'

'He needs more toys.'

'He cannot play with toys, they defeat him. A stuffed rabbit is his enemy, but tins he understands. He is preparing for adult life. He will be a collector of art or money or women. Or he will become a squirrel.'

'Your soup's burning.'

He hurried back to the stove as Toplady came down the garden carrying what looked like a square package. He was very damp, when he came close the animal kingdom smelled woolly, leathery, meaty. The rain was laying out big spots like a careful gambler.

Toplady swept past Boris who was on his knees mopping up soup. What I had thought was a package turned out to be a wooden panel. He propped it against the hall table and I saw that it was one of Maria's paintings.

'Where did you find that?'

'In the bushes. It's about the right size to fill a gap in my back-yard fence.'

'It's a painting.'

'You don't say.' He bent to look. 'Certainly someone's sloshed paint on it.'

'It belongs to Maria Odenda, an artist who lives here.'

He made for our front room. I call it that because it has the same purpose as a front man, it preserves anonymity. I keep a grape-ivy in the window, everyone grows grape-ivies. Toplady's briefcase I now saw bore the inscription 'PEN International Congress'.

'What does PEN stand for?'

'Poets, Editors and Novelists. It's a world-wide affiliation of writers.'

'Could I join?'

'Only published writers are eligible.'

'I'll join when I'm published. Perhaps they'd take over this house.'

'They already have a house.'

'I've got to do something.' I saw his ears move, they didn't prick, they shot forward. 'I can't afford to keep the house going on the present basis. I need to let every room. I want to let to writers, make it a creative centre.'

'Writers don't centralize.'

'What about PEN writers?'

'Professionals. They meet in Chelsea and travel all over to conferences and congresses. They stay in International Hiltons and talk turkey to foreign governments. You'd never get their sort here.'

'I want creative writers, I don't mind whether they've been published or not.'

'You're nothing till you get into print.'

'I've already won a big literary award.'

'As big as the Booker?'

'It was a literary valuation, not a commercial hype. I'm currently researching for my book about Napoleon.'

'Did you know someone's just brought out a book written as if it's his horse talking?'

'The Hogarth Press are pressing me to sign a contract with them.'

'Vanity presses are after your money. If you've got any, invest it.'

'Look,' I said, 'are you a publisher or aren't you?'

He pulled up his chair close to mine. 'You've heard of Beauty and the Beast?'

For a wild moment I thought he was alluding to himself and me. 'Of course.'

'Little Red Riding Hood? Goldilocks and the Three Bears? Cinderella?'

'They're fairy-tales.'

'Hairy tales.'

'Written by the German brothers Grimm, and Hans Andersen – he was Danish.' I supposed he was putting me through a general knowledge test. 'Based on folklore and old ballads.'

'Could you re-write them?'

'Not my field.'

'Nor is history. You should be writing about people of your own time.'

'You mean Red Riding Hood and Goldilocks?'

'Let me tell you about my little enterprise. Myself and friends have set up a company to produce videos for private showing. We have the talent, professional actors working in their spare time: we have cameraman and editor, unemployed but clawing their way back. At present we're in it for less than peanuts, but it's only the beginning. We're shooting re-writes of classic stories: *Sinella* and *Blondie and the Huggy Bears*, old stuff with a new slant, artistically presented and very zesty.'

'Zesty?'

'Full of human interest. Know what I mean?'

'Human interest is the criterion of good fiction.'

96

'What would you say is the universal sphere of human interest?'

'I suppose – love.' I had to suppose that. I said, to put off a discussion, 'There are so many kinds, it's a very complex subject.'

'Sex is your universal sphere. Every man, woman and bug is hung up on sex. I'll run a sequence for you and you can try scripting it. Make no mistake, the visuals are explicit, we just want a few well-chosen words for the benefit of those who like everything spelled out. Myself, I prefer subtlety.'

'I shan't have time.'

'Take my advice, forget literature. The future's in videos. Why shouldn't basic encounters make quality visuals – video-niceys? Our team's got the imagination, all we need is some documentary, real-life asides taken from your own experience.' He approached, the same peppered nose which had topped me in Mrs Spilsbury's bed. 'As I recall you didn't have much at our basic encounter. Was it like dancing, you said.'

'I re-create, re-cycle people,' there'll be some of my father and a lot of Maria in my Napoleon, 'and places I've been to.' I've been to the Palm House at Kew. They used to have a Napoleon willow there, but it died. At Eastbourne I watch the sea come in over cold grey stones, I give my mind to it and I'm on St Helena.

'We're interpreting the classics. Each story will have a distinctive slant – cultural, political, scientific, psychological. You'd be surprised what psychology there is in Red Riding Hood. Another thing: this house has potential. In this room there's plenty of space and a good high ceiling. Take up the mats and we'll have a floor for tracking. And that fragmented light from the leaded windows we can use. Not the furniture though, it won't do for dog-shots.'

'Why don't you film in your own house?'

'I haven't got a house, just a ground-floor flat and a yard.'

'Are you married?'

'Thank Christ no. You don't know how lucky you are.'

'Not being married?'

'Living here. They don't build like this any more. This house has style, individuality. Of course for the palace scenes we have

97

to have a big staircase. We've got Stackpole Hall, Sinella runs down like a frightened deer –'

'A deer – on stairs?'

'She knows she's going to lose her party clothes if she doesn't get clear before the clock finishes striking midnight. So the striptease starts at the top of the stairs and by the time she's got to the bottom she's starkers. There follows a comic sequence with the Ugly Sisters trying to get into her bra.'

I was in a position to count the pocks on his nose. I don't believe that story he told about the key and the gunpowder, I think he caught something. Like Plague.

'I've had a look at that mini rain-forest at the back.'

'My garden?'

'It's just how Bluebeard's would be after a hundred years without a mower.'

'It was the garden of the Sleeping Beauty's castle that hadn't been touched for a hundred years.'

'We'll use a bit of this and cut into a bit of that. It's called technique, what filming's about.'

'I thought you were a publisher, Victor Gollancz or someone, and we'd talk about my book.'

'You haven't written a book.'

'I need time to write it.'

'Ever thought of buying time?' He picked up his briefcase and went to the door. In the hall he took up Maria's picture.

'You can't have that,' I said. 'It belongs to Maria.'

He waved and went without looking round.

Nell came flying downstairs in what she calls her peignoir, blue silk with swansdown ruffles. I told her she looked like Sinella.

'Who?'

'Never mind.'

'Boris said there was a publisher here – have you signed a contract?'

'I'm thinking about it.'

'Tell me what he said.'

'He wants me to do a film script.'

'Of your book? Zeph, that's terrific – you're made!'

98

'My book's not even written and probably never will be.' I shocked myself saying that, but Nell was the only one who wouldn't believe it. I was on rock-bottom and trying to get my foot off.

'If you do the film of the book you won't even need to write the book.'

'I want to write the book!'

'You can write all the books you want once you've made some money. The chicken comes before the egg.'

'My work doesn't lend itself to visual interpretation.'

'It's too soon for you to be playing hard to get. Zeph, you've got to start selling yourself.'

'I can't write porn.'

'Do you have to?'

'That man doesn't publish books, he makes blue videos out of fairy-tales.'

'Zowie!' I saw understanding dawning – 'You mean like Beauty and the Beast?' – shaping and emulsifying – 'Snow White and the Seven Dwarves?'

'Dwarfs.'

'Making raunchy videos could be instructive.'

'That sort of thing makes me sick.'

'You need to learn about sex. You don't know enough, it bothers me.'

'Does it? Does it really!'

'You'd get valuable insight into the workings of human nature. Men's, in particular. Your Napoleon would have loved blue videos on St Helena.'

'What I need is time and contributory ambience. I won't get that by corrupting my inspiration with Toplady's dirty pictures.'

'Whose?'

'His name's Toplady, but it's more a question of what he'd like to do than what he can do.' My mother hadn't appreciated Dick Spilsbury's crack. She wanted me to have a real life but the reality had to be to her taste so she could join in. 'You know what's a real laugh? The one writer who lives in this writers' house can't write!'

'Cheer up, childie.' Nell put her arm round me. 'Boris is doing a symbolic sculpture for your front garden which will bring in the glitteraties.'

I, the writer, am prevented by force of circumstance. The force doesn't have to be graded to the circumstance. It can be big and national, like getting imprisoned for dissidence: mine's just as forceful though it's simply the circumstance of having to earn what doesn't even amount to a living. Here am I, wasting time all the time. My life is slipping away, taking my life's work with it. Every day another thousand words are lost.

When I think of the centuries wasted by people who are just passing through life on their way to oblivion, filling their time with shopping and jogging, I feel savage. I think of the Lady of Shalott on her island, nothing to do but watch the boats. I could use what she had – solitude, peace, *time*, I wouldn't even see the boats.

I went to the library and asked what they had on Napoleon. They said of course he was in all the encyclopedias, histories, biographies, lives of conquerors, the Dictionary of International Biography, and they thought there was an analysis of his bumps in a phrenological study of famous men. Besides all that, their computer-thingy said they had three plays and five novels. As our library usually only stocks two per cent of anything I reckoned there could be at least a hundred novels already in print. I needed to talk to someone. I asked Maria if she had seen Montrose.

'Never see him now.'

Diggory was in her lap, staring into her face with the energy he puts into his movements.

'Is he still living in Sydenham?'

'I'm never going back there.'

'It's a mistake to go back to a place where you were happy.'

'I was happy, Edgar wasn't. It wasn't real happiness because it wasn't shared.'

With an outlook like that she should go into a nunnery. 'You're over-reacting.'

'I thought if I could be everything she wasn't, I'd be right for him.'

'Of course he told you everything she wasn't. Perhaps you'll tell me what she was, just for the record.'

Shakespeare wrote that the evil men do lives after them. It wasn't evil my mother did, but I tend to remember the bad things. Like he said, the poet's imagination gives substance to thoughts we don't want to have, but ought to.

Diggory growled low-key. 'He wants a story.'

'So do I.'

'Can't think of anything to interest you.'

'Everything interests a writer.'

Diggory shouted, 'A Nancy!'

I was startled, never having heard him use words. He bounced vigorously in Maria's lap. She dumped him on the floor and he howled like a police klaxon.

'Make him stop that.'

She put her hand over his mouth. 'Hush up, honey, and I'll tell you a Tiger story.'

He climbed back into her lap, knelt and gazed into her face.

'Isn't there a story about my mother?' I said.

'That's not for me to tell nor for you to be told.'

'She's gone, he's gone, you're the only one who can tell me. You could, couldn't you?'

'Some things you got to find out yourself.'

'I can only do that from you.'

'Give it some time. You come to me in five, maybe ten years, and you still don't know, I'll have a story for you.'

Diggory's chest could be seen filling for another howling session.

'Okay, honey, here's a story for you. Once Tiger ruled the forest, Tiger was king, his name on everything stripey, tiger-lilies, tiger-moths, tiger-nuts, tiger-snakes. He had the best teeth in the business and liked to eat people. But Anansi, the Spider, was smarter. For one thing he had four times as many legs and could run rings round the lightning. Also he could change himself into people – and that made Tiger's mouth water. Then so soon as Tiger got ready to pounce, Anansi would change back into a spider and run away on all his legs.

101

'One day Tiger found a honey-hole in a tree-stump. His teeth were sweet and while the bees were away he ate up their honey. Then he went to Anansi and said he knew of this hole with more honey in it than anybody could eat. Anansi didn't want to get his legs dirty. Tiger said what a pity you don't have fingers, guess I'll have to try and eat some more. He groaned and patted his belly to show how full he was. Anansi followed him back to the hole, Tiger lay down under a tree and pretended to go to sleep. Anansi came to the hole and changed himself into a fat man and stuck his fingers into the tree-stump.

'Tiger sprang, but the bees were come home and they flew into his face and blinded him. They would have stung Anansi but he had turned back into a spider and ran away to his web.'

Ethnic culture gives me a feeling that everything I'm trying to say is in square one and has all been said.

'What's it supposed to mean?'

'It's an old Carib story. Caribs lived on the moon till they looked down and saw our nice things. Guess it means it's more fun on the earth.'

When I saw Toplady paying off a cab at my gate, here we *aren't* going again I thought, and put on my coat. He had a girl with him, and a suitcase. I let them get as far as the porch, then I opened the door and said I was just going out.

'We'll wait.' He planted the suitcase on the mat inside the door.

'I shall be a long time.'

'We've got time.'

'I shan't be back until tomorrow.'

'I need the toilet,' said the girl.

'I'm sorry –'

'I need it now.' She started to dance.

'Meet Sister Sophie,' said Toplady.

The girl cried, 'For God's sake, where is it?'

I pointed to the downstairs cloaks, she rushed in and slammed the door. 'I have to go,' I said, 'I'm seeing a man about my book.'

'Never rush to see a publisher, it's a sign you're up for grabs.'

'I'm late already.'

102

'Keep him waiting, he'll respect you for it.' He brought the suitcase into the hall. 'Come in and let's talk.'

'I don't want to.'

'It's to your advantage.' He called, 'We're in the back, Sophie,' and went through to the kitchen.

I had to follow. He leaned over the sink, looking out of the window. 'Got any more of those boards?'

'Boards?'

'Like the one I took the other day.'

'That was a painting.'

'It was?'

'One of Maria Odenda's. She lives upstairs.'

'I used it to patch my fence. It was fine. There are still some gaps so I thought I'd pick up two or three more.'

'You can't. The one you took had been carried into the garden by mistake. It belongs to Maria.'

'Pity.'

'Who's the girl?'

'Our female lead. Sophie's got the carriage of a queen and she can sit on her hair.'

'Why has she brought her luggage?'

'She needs a room.'

'No.'

'While we're shooting the last of *Sinella*.'

'No.'

'For a couple of weeks, maybe less. You can do with the money.'

'I haven't a room free.'

'She's a lovely girl, you'll love her.'

She *is* lovely, big and bloomy like the women who sit on clouds in the National Gallery. She called 'Cooee!' along the passage and came to the doorway patting between her legs. 'Call of nature, I was getting so I couldn't think. By the by, your flush takes a lot of coaxing.'

'It never works till the third push.'

'I'll know in future.'

'Look,' I said, 'about the future –'

'This Maria, what does she do?'

'Paints.'

103

'Does she sell?'

'I don't know.'

'Well, I'll take a few more boards off her hands.'

'I like it here,' said Sophie. 'When do I get to see my room?'

'Sophie writes,' said Toplady. 'She's scripting *Sinella* for us.'

Sophie reached into her dress and scratched between her bosoms, a gesture of disassociation if ever I saw one. Toplady said something under his breath. I had expected those two to be close, hand in glove, hand in hand anyway, lovers, I thought, a conclusion which I had passed rather than come to. It turns out they may be hand in glove but they're not hand in hand. I suppose that's another aspect of sex: you can be a love-maker and make only a fuss.

I said, 'Can you really sit on your hair?'

She laughed. 'I'd break my neck if I tried.'

Toplady asked where Maria's room was. 'I'll go and see her.'

'What for?'

'To discuss the going rate for packing-cases.'

Sophie was re-pinning her hair and didn't meet my eye. Toplady moved to the door but I got there first. 'Maria won't see you without an appointment, she's funny about her work.'

'I can understand that.' He grinned.

'What about the room?' said Sophie. 'Are there cooking facilities?'

'There's use of the kitchen at stated times.'

'I'll give you fifty a week,' said Toplady, 'inclusive of VAT.'

I gave her the room next to mine. I remember my father occupying it once. He locked the door and wouldn't open. My mother sent me. I was seven years old. He looked at me through the keyhole. His eye was like a jelly-bean. I asked were we playing hide and seek. My mother said, 'He has a headache.'

But it's a pleasant room with a view of Stackpole Hall. In winter when the trees are bare you can see the lake. I left a crocheted hair-tidy on the dressing-table mirror, I thought Sophie would find it useful.

'Look at that lake! Imagine seeing a lake from my window! Where's the bathroom?'

'Across the passage.'

'I'll take it.'

'You'll have to lock your door if you don't want to be disturbed.' She was pinning her hair up, it's the colour of lemons and she has trouble keeping it up. She said she wasn't disturbable.

'Someone wanders around the house.'

'Male or female?'

'Male.'

'Under sixty he'll be welcome.'

'He's under three.'

'What is he? A dog?'

'A child. Don't be surprised if you find him under your bed.'

'A baby?' She sounded pleased. 'Whose?'

'Nell's and Boris's, they have the room on the next landing.'

'Do they write?'

'Boris is a sculptor, Nell was at school with me. They'll go when they find a place of their own.'

'Then you'll get some lodgers.'

'I don't want lodgers, I want writers, people I can talk to about writing and who will talk to me. I don't care what their genres are so long as they're genuinely innovative.' Sophie gazed into the mirror, arms upheld, hands outspread. She'd look wonderful carved in stone, holding up a roof. 'I've no head for pornography.'

'It's not all mental though, is it? I was hoping you'd show me how to make the connection. You'd have to promise your writers wine and cheese.'

'I can't afford wine and cheese.'

'And a captive audience for regular readings from their work.'

'Where would I get a captive audience?'

'From the writers. They'll all be waiting their turn to read.'

'You can put your combings in the tidy.'

'Isn't it something! Hand-done, isn't it?' She held up a tress of hair, measuring the length. She couldn't have sat on it. 'Tell your friend he got twenty guineas for her picture.'

'Maria's? I don't believe it. Her work's highly personal. She's experimenting, mucking about with paint. She puts it on thick and sticky. Who would want to buy a picture of jam butty without the butty?'

Maria didn't believe it either, 'That's crazy!'
   'Sophie says you can sell anything if you know where to take it. I mean any sort of thing, it could be thimbles or teddy-bears.'
   'If she comes to live here this house is going to be full of crazy people.'
   'You shouldn't underestimate your gift.'
   'I'm talking about that man in your momma's room, skins a chicken and calls it Art.'
   'If your picture fetched any money you should get it.'
   'Twenty guineas for one picture? There's more where that came from, there's forever more.'
   'Don't let him think that.'
   'What's he got to think?'
   'That you haven't painted many pictures and you don't want to part with them. He's found somewhere to sell your work and he'll try to cheat you out of the money.'
   'I should get there first.'
   'We don't even know if the price is fair.'
   'I've got two – three dozen pictures, if I get twenty-one pounds for every one I'm going to be rich!'
   'He'll tell you your work's only worth it's the woodpainted on.'
   'Okay, so I'll sell him the bits I haven't painted on. They're so clean and pure I'll ask twenty-five pounds apiece.' Maria giggled. 'There's a box had Tuna Chunks in, five lovely panels. Don't you fret, I can handle him. I handled Aunt Luella, there was no one meaner with money than her.'

Sophie has a point. I put another card in the corner-shop window: 'Rooms to let in writer's house. Regular reading and discussion sessions in creative atmosphere: dedication and spiritual refreshment'. They mustn't think refreshment meant wine and cheese.
   I had to redefine my perspectives, you could say refine them. Five thousand novels were published last year, some people can't write anything else.

I've thought a lot about the relationship of poetry to prose. One day in class I asked Miss Abercorn which was the greater work – in her opinion, I was careful to say – 'Ode to a Nightingale' or *Jane Eyre*. She said surely it depended on which had the most words. As she never made jokes nobody laughed and she blamed me.

Now I can see past the sarcasm to what she really meant. I wish she could know I've seen it. At last. It *is* a question of words. They have to be chosen, like pearls, each for its rightness. A poem is a ring of words. It holds the greatest truth, a universal one which is true whichever way you look at it. That's a big order, you don't get any bigger with an eighty-thousand-word novel, you just eke out.

My novels will have the minimum of words and the maximum of meaning – poetic fictions, blending poetry and prose. Word perfection is what I'm after. I shall discipline myself. Inspiration is divine intervention and I've been chosen to be intervened. But I also have to exercise a choice, and I do mean *exercise*.

History's not my thing: Napoleon, St Helena and those he-and-she cabbage-trees. That's why I couldn't get started, why I've been wasting the little time I have.

My ideas about people were elementary. I hoped that Nell and Sophie would take to each other and become friends – I didn't go any farther than that. When I introduced them all, Sophie and Nell, Sophie and Boris, Sophie and Diggory, there was a sort of electrical arcing. And a junior spark from Diggory which Sophie returned, scooping him up with adoring cries. He's still wearing Pampers and even environment-friendly can become unfriendly after it's been crawling around the house all day. Seeing him pressed to Sophie's beautiful bosom was heartwarming.

'Sophie will be staying with us for a while,' I said. 'She writes.'

Nell said, 'Hi.'

'She also acts. On films.'

'Stage,' said Sophie. 'We don't count videos.'

Boris bowed from the waist and kissed his hand to Sophie.

He couldn't kiss hers, they were clasped under Diggory's bottom.

She said, 'How I envy you this little boy!'

'Will you sit for me?' Boris said.

'He's a sculptor,' said Nell, 'he'd like to do your bust.'

Sophie uttered a deep delicious gurgle. Diggory, enchanted with the sound, tried to catch it in her throat. 'My little beau!' She rubbed noses with him and he choked with emotion.

'Maria will be jealous,' I said.

Nell said, 'Maria had a little tot, he was white, she was not.'

Boris went to Sophie and made shapes with his hands: squares, circles and chinks which he squinneyed through, sizing her up I supposed.

I said, 'You know you can't sculpt stone in the house.'

'I shall do a maquette in clay.'

Sophie said, 'Afraid I won't have time to sit.'

'Put the child down, he interrupts the line of view.'

Diggory clung with arms round Sophie's neck and his legs round her waist. She cuddled him, smiling.

The look Nell gave Boris's back positively sparked. She plucked Diggory out of Sophie's grasp. He beat punily and silently at the air.

'Poor lamb,' said Sophie.

'I wish to cast you in bronze.' Boris circled to get a rear view.

'Won't that take hours? We're on such a tight schedule. It's extraordinarily difficult to get everyone together on two consecutive days. Or even one day with people not in regular work, doing this and that to keep their heads above water.'

'What parts do you take?' Diggory tried to squirm off Nell's lap but she held him under his armpits. His clothes parted company and showed his navel.

'Sophie's the romantic lead,' I said.

'They'd like me to do make-up as well. I do my own but I can't cope with the Beast's. Dalton wants him with a lion's mane, an elephant's trunk and shark's teeth.'

I suggested they use a Japanese fright-mask, it would save time and trouble and could be slipped off in the transformation scene.

'Dalton wants make-up melting in full view of the camera, like *Death in Venice*. He's pulling out all the stops. He thinks religion stimulates arousal. I'm billed as Sister Sophie in a wimpole.'

'Wimple.'

Nell said, 'Sounds like fun.' Diggory wept and Boris informed Sophie that she was a poet because there was poetry in her face and form. I said you didn't have to be beautiful to write beautifully, look at Philip Larkin. Boris said he was talking about the quality of beauty.

I looked at Nell. Boris looked at Sophie. Nell mopped Diggory's tears. 'Who is this Dalton?'

'Dalton Toplady. Runs a private limited company making specialized videos.'

'Blue movies,' I said. 'I don't mind about the porn but I do mind him cheating Maria over her pictures.'

'He's transparent,' said Sophie. 'She'll see through him.'

'If cheating people is what he wants to do yet he's no good at it, that doesn't make him any better.'

'I'm the wrong one to ask about morals. Never know what they are.'

'Maria can take care of herself,' said Nell.

'He's soft. You'd be surprised how soft in the middle he is.'

Sophie spoke directly to Boris, smiling at him. Nell went on mopping Diggory and did not look at any of us.

Toplady's soft spot must be brown rotten. He came next day and asked me what I thought of Sophie. I said I didn't think anything, she'd only been in the house overnight.

'She's like you, got a vivid imagination. Don't believe everything she tells you. Mind you, she's not a liar, just a good wholesome girl.'

I remembered her saying she didn't know what morals are and thought I wouldn't have to work at character analysis because people are so screwed up anything goes.

'But when it comes to real life . . .' He shrugged. The business he's in, he's a fine one to talk about real life, he must be the finest because there's nothing so real as dirt. 'Money, for instance, she's no good with money.'

'Are you telling me she can't pay her rent?'

'No problem there. It's the unit I'm referring to.'

'What unit?'

'The film unit. I'm talking about our finances.'

'Why talk to me about that?'

'What I'm saying is, any new business has to take a running jump to get started. Sophie doesn't understand that there's a risk element, especially in the entertainment game. But in our particular branch the risk is minimized. We're providing a needed service to people under pressure. We all need releases, it's like going to confession. Watching porn liberates the secret thoughts.'

'Not mine.'

He gently teased his whiskers but they didn't want to play, they sulked. 'So you're determined to write a book and you've got to fund it and you're making – what? Six per cent net with instant access from Abbey National. Ever thought of diversifying? Investing for your future instead of for unknown mortgagees?'

'I haven't any money in Abbey National.'

'You've got this house. It's nice, but houses fall to bits while you're not looking: damp-rot, dry-rot, woodworm, subsidence, cracked walls, toadstools in the loft.'

'I haven't got toadstools in my loft.'

'So sell it. Invest the money and buy time to write your book.'

'I don't want to sell.'

'Vizzies are here to stay. In a year from now sixty per cent of the population of the British Isles, currently standing at fifty-seven and a half million, will be running their own shows, catering for their individual tastes. That's quite a market demand, you could be in at the beginning.'

'While we're on the subject of money, what about Maria?'

'What about who?'

'You sold a picture of hers for twenty guineas. Allowing ten per cent commission which you're not entitled to because it was sold without her consent, it makes you owe her eighteen pounds, ninety.'

'You heard that from Sophie.' He sighed. 'It's wishful think-ing.'

'I believe her.'

'Sophie will say anything to make you happy.'

'It made Maria happy.'

'Sophie wants everyone happy. I keep telling her pretending won't make it work. It didn't for us.'

'You?'

'There was a time when I thought she felt something for me. She let me think so.'

'You were doing the wishful.'

'There she was, pretty girl, devoted to me. She made this old war-horse very happy. But to her every man's a big cuddle. The bottom fell out of my world when I realized it. It broke my heart.'

They say you only tell the truth in clichés because the truth is a cliché. I looked into Toplady's eyes and we achieved a frontier clash.

'You've got to talk to Maria about the money you owe her for her painting.'

He sighed again, causing a furore among his nose-hairs. 'Painting d'you call it? Is she stoned or something? Where would I get twenty-one smackers for that gizmo? You can go into a shop and buy lovely nudes and mutant turtles ready-framed for under a fiver.'

'Maria's an original artist, there's only one of that painting in existence.'

'Thank Christ. I'll talk to her.'

'Now?'

'I haven't done talking to you.'

'I've done listening.'

He stood up with one uneasy movement and came close, bringing his face two centimetres from mine. I knew that something unprovoked was about to happen and I counted the pocks on his nose while I waited. Twenty-one.

What happened was he tried to kiss me. He seized me by the shoulders and snatched me to him. We were back in Mrs Spilsbury's bed. He didn't have much technique and I spoiled what he had. I wrenched my head aside so that his mouth skidded off mine and down my cheek. There was so much force, passion or predestination behind it that he couldn't halt the descent and ended by getting a poke in the eye from the back of my chair. While he was nursing it, I ducked under his arm and put the chair between us.

He glared at me through a welter of tears. 'What's the matter with you?'

'I don't feel like it.'

'You never do, you never have.'

'I'm not in favour of distributive sex.'

'You're not normal. What sort of book do you expect to write with your libido in deep freeze?' The truth was I couldn't fancy him, but feeling responsible for his eye, didn't like to tell him so. 'Baby stories is all you're capable of.' He was starting to sneer. 'And babies know more about sex than you do.'

'You're quite wrong. Fieldwork's not necessary if you have sufficient imaginative range.'

'Christ, this hurts – I'll have a black eye!'

'You should put steak on it. Afraid I only have corned beef.'

He threw a five-pound note on the table. 'Give this to your Maria, it's what I got for her picture.'

I wrote a poem. It was good, how do you write bad poetry? Poetry's apocalyptic, it comes to you. A Voice spoke to me, whispering words from somewhere private, riches I didn't know I possessed.

I believe in miracles: if this one could happen, so could others, people could be raised from the dead, let alone such simple ploys as changing water into wine.

When I think how I agonized over Napoleon – who was it who was doomed to push a big stone up a mountain and have it roll back every time he got near the top? I know the feeling, I was pushing a big book.

This poem came to me and I got the words down, no trouble with sequence, they followed each other like a chime of bells. The meaning was something I've been wanting to tell the world but could never express. Truth isn't a cliché, it can only be expressed in poetry, it has to be *divined*. Small wonder that when I got anything together it was about as riveting as the Yellow Pages.

My poem was an idyll about nature, the natural order as it relates to us, as we'd like it to relate. Well, most of us would. I heard someone at the funeral say that the way she died, quick and tidy, was the best way to go. It wasn't so tidy because of the eggs and the bag of flour she was carrying. But my poem embalmed the thought without being morbid or hypochondriacal.

Prose is laid flat on the page, the reader has to work to make something of it. And gets it wrong half the time. Poetry springs right off the page, and when it's spoken aloud in the poet's voice it comes straight from the poet's heart.

I wrote about the quiet life and how nice to live it: about transience and wanting to be a vegetable. There were implications, organic, environmental, ethical, economic, in my poem. It could have taken thousands of words to put over such a theme. I did it in one hundred and thirty-nine.

You don't question the creative will, you can't bring it on, or stop it, it's like weather, you take what comes. Of course I had to tidy up the iambics, that's the poet's job. The result was a universal truth in a form designed to stimulate lateral thinking.

I recited it to my Iris Murdochs, I wanted to give it to the world. I was in the blaze which goes unheeded by non-creators. I thought if only I had my writers' circle.

I had Nell and Maria and Sophie and Boris. 'I'd like us all to get together one evening.'

'A swurry?' said Nell.

'A discussion. To talk about our work.'

'I don't have any work, unless you want to hear about amino acids and E numbers.'

'I want your opinion of something I've written. Boris can talk about his sculpture, Maria about her paintings, and Sophie about her video-scripts. We'll benefit from each other's point of view.'

'Depends which way it's pointing.'

'Thursday, eight o'clock in our front room.'

'How's the Corsican coming along?'

'It was a mistake. I'm not going to do that book. I'm concentrating on metrical composition.'

'You're writing music?'

'The music of words.'

'We always eat around eight.'

'We'll make it half-past. There'll be wine and cheese.'

I invited Montrose. He said he didn't know if he could come. 'Please,' I said, 'it's vitally important that you're there when I read my work.'

'Why so?'

'Because it's the first thing I've finished.'

I cut the cheese into cubes and spiked them on toothpicks as I'd seen it done for a wine-tasting in Tesco. Maria put on a black and green kaftan for the occasion, it made her look like an aubergine. Sophie did her hair over a pad, in a sort of tower, yellow as brass and looking as solid. Nell came in her working-clothes, jeans and Sloppy Joe, she never makes up now, she doesn't need to, she has an interesting bone-structure. Boris brought something in a Big Shopper.

'You haven't brought any of your paintings,' I said to Maria, 'so we could look at it and talk about it – I told you we were going to have a discussion.'

'Nothing to discuss.'

She shrugged and the kaftan squawked. 'That's a noisy dress,' I said. Boris cuddled the Big Shopper and gazed at Sophie who had taken a toothpick out of a piece of cheese and was working on her quicks.

'I am ready to begin,' he said.

I said, 'We must wait for Montrose.'

Sophie asked what he wrote. 'He's a literary critic, I value his opinion.'

Maria's eye rolled. Sophie put the toothpick back in the cheese. Boris commented that critics were failed artists.

'You can't say that about Anthony Burgess, A.S. Byatt, Virginia Woolf.'

'Have I said it? Who are these people?'

'They're writers, tovarish,' said Nell.

'In the manipulative arts failure is not achieved, it manifests itself.'

Maria said she didn't want to hear about failure and Boris said he was talking about success which was immediately evident or absent in the work of a man's hands.

'Men have the biggest thumbs,' said Maria.

Boris said he wasn't talking about sexual discrimination but about mankind.

'Personkind,' said Nell. Sophie laughed. Maria said women didn't signify. I said, 'You don't really think that,' and she said no, she knew it. I said what about Mrs Thatcher, she signified to just about everyone. Maria said who was talking about government? 'Look,' I started to say and she said, '*You* look. I'm talking about me, I work with my hands, I paint like crazy, the man said. Pictures? he said, You call those pictures?'

'What man?'

'You didn't let him have anything I hope,' said Sophie.

Maria grinned. 'He thinks he's so clever, like Anansi, got all his wits. I've got mine too. He said he'd take a couple of boards to patch his fence. I said colours wouldn't look good in it and he could have some unpainted boxes for twenty pounds a time. He said he'd have to go and measure the holes.'

'He'll be back,' said Sophie. 'He's found someone interested enough in your work to pay for it.'

'Nobody wants my pictures. I took a couple to a place in the High Street for sale or return. They said no thank you, so I gave them to the Charity Shop. They put them in the back with the old shoes.'

'Try the galleries, someone's sure to be into ethnic art,' said Sophie.

Montrose hadn't come. Nell opened the wine. Sophie sat at Boris's feet and gazed up at him as if he was a guru. 'Tell me about your work.'

He put the Big Shopper on the floor and stroked her neck, unlike a guru. I hoped they'd keep it private, I didn't want to hear about his work.

Nell handed Maria a glass of Lambrusco. 'Do you really see what you paint, everything on a collision course?'

'I don't do easel pictures.'

'I saw box-art in the States, but nothing like your splinter-work.' Nell took a sip of wine and shuddered. 'Who's Anansi?'

'A spider. A big black male with hairy legs.'

'Spiders are female, they eat the males.'

Maria said scornfully, 'If women spiders eat men spiders how do baby spiders get born?'

115

'It's a post-coital reaction, we all have different ones. Spiders eat each other, I eat candy-bars. What about you?'

Nell put the question as she might enquire what soap powder Maria used, except that that was something Nell would never ask. But it got to Maria: she didn't colour up, she did the only thing she could, she *dis*coloured, pale beige. I could see that Nell was using her for something else. The corner of her eye was on Sophie, Sophie leaned ever deeper into Boris's bifurcation. He was bending over her, his East European curls vibrating. I remembered Toplady saying that to Sophie every man was a big cuddle. I'm learning to push my narrative tendency, maybe it's what Maria meant when she said there were things I ought to find out for myself.

Maria said, 'What are we here for?' She despised us – Boris and Sophie and Nell and me – me especially because we were supposed to be having a meeting and I was supposed to be keeping order.

'I'm here to be read to,' said Nell, 'from Zeph's latest work. How much longer must we wait?'

'Can't be too long for some,' Maria said tartly, watching Sophie clasped between Boris's thighs.

Nell laughed her cadence laugh, extra mellifluous. She was juggling with the situation, it must take a special knack to throw up your husband and another woman and finish with them both in your hands.

Sophie suddenly turned away from Boris and looked at Nell, and Nell looked down at her. It's a moment which comes early in the *How to Write Successful Fiction Guide*: What is the eternal triangle? Why is it so called? Give examples in literature.

I said, 'Sophie, tell us how you write your video-scripts. Where do you find your inspiration?'

'My what?'

'Look, we're not here to shilly-shally –' I might have put it more strongly, 'we're here to give honest and helpful opinions about each other's work.'

Boris said the artist was the first judge, he alone knew what he had purposed and if it had been achieved. I was inclined to agree, but reminded him that Art is Communication, a bridge of minds. I liked the phrase. 'We're islands,' I said, 'without a Bridge of Minds.'

'Sweetie, by no stretch of imagination can my video-scripts be called Art.'

'Black art perhaps?' said Nell.

It's the sort of thing you say without thinking, or if you're thinking some other thing. Present company excepted, someone should have said. But Nell wasn't thinking about Maria, she'd forgotten Maria was present. She was thinking about Sophie and Boris her husband, and herself. There was a lot of scope, that's why it's called 'eternal'.

Sophie put an elbow on each of Boris's knees and uncoiled like a cat and stood up to confront Nell. She smiled, Nell didn't. It was a big moment.

I said, 'The old fairy-tales are black. People are chopped to bits, fattened for witches' dinners and beautiful princesses marry monsters.'

'Better marry than be eaten by a crocodile,' said Maria.

'You're into a grey area,' said Nell.

Sophie laughed and again Nell didn't. The evening wasn't turning out at all as I'd intended. The eternal triangle was blocking intelligent discourse. I tapped on a wine-glass and said briskly, 'Do we believe in Art as Communication? I believe we must, if we paint or sculpt or write. And if we don't, if we're just receivers, we must be ready to say what we receive.' I turned to Maria. 'Why do you paint?'

She shrugged. 'Paint and brush make bad things come.'

'What bad things?'

'You ask damn silly questions.'

'I want to find out about Art, why we do it, what it *is*. I believe it's deep deep understanding invested in the artist, it's one-ness. Art is the union of sensibilities.' That was the biggest moment, absolute truth was raying out of me, I felt effulgent.

I looked round at them to see how far it had penetrated. Boris was untouched, Nell put up her thumb and forefinger in a gesture of admiration, Sophie glowed pink and gold. But I couldn't take credit for that.

Maria said, 'I used to paint nice things. Not any more.'

'Why not?'

'You should know.'

I said 'I'm trying to establish the concept of Art as Communication.'

'The telephone communicates, the artist sublimates,' said Boris.

'When I was happy I painted nice things,' said Maria. 'Now I paint the sweet-voiced crocodile.'

'The what?'

'My Aunt Luella said we should learn we had to take trouble to get what we wanted. She told us about a man had a pretty daughter and made her so comfortable she didn't want to marry and leave home. He got tired opening the door to young men who kept coming courting and hid the girl in a house by the river. He said to admit nobody but her mother who would bring food and sing a song to identify her.

    ' "Leah, Leah, ting-aling-ling
       Honey at the door, darling,
       Sugar at the door, darling,
       Leah, Leah, ting-aling-ling."

'A crocodile was listening and memorized the song. Next morning early he went and sang it, figuring the girl would come for her breakfast. But she knew the voice wasn't her mother's and didn't open the door. So the crocodile had the blacksmith tenderize his vocal chord with a red-hot nail. The blacksmith told him so long as his throat was raw he'd sing like a nightingale. But the operation was painful, the crocodile ate some mangoes to soothe his throat. Right away he lost his sweet voice and brayed like a donkey. He went back to the blacksmith who took out his tonsils with red-hot pinchers. The crocodile rushed round to the girl's house and sang "Honey at the door, darling," in a sweet voice and a lot of pain. She opened the door and he gobbled her up. All but her shoes.'

'He was a fussy eater?' said Sophie.

'Her shoes were crocodile leather, he wasn't a cannibal.'

'If that's the sort of story you tell my child, no wonder he has nightmares,' said Nell.

118

'Aunt Luella heard it from her grandmother in Haiti.'

'Dalton would make it into a video,' said Sophie.

'The machine as artist,' Boris said bitterly.

Nell said, 'I think I'll go to bed.'

'Please – you haven't heard my poem.'

'Go ahead, read it.'

Luckily for me (I thought it was at the time) Montrose arrived. I thought it will be all right now, I'll read my poem, they'll all listen and he'll say what he thinks of it. I experienced a sharp intestinal qualm, followed by an upsurge of faith. Some people put theirs in God, mine's in my inspiration. The same thing really.

For Sophie, Montrose was a new encounter. As a writer my task is to explore and select and transmute: it would be fruitless – or rather it would be the same old fruit – if I didn't select. Montrose and Sophie are poles apart: south and west – you never hear of a West Pole, but there must be one – they have a lot of the same culture, only Montrose has ethnicity. I could foresee psychological complexities, character structures and big plot diversions. I introduced him as Montrose Odenda, student and critic of English literature.

'Critic?' said Nell.

'My brother,' said Maria.

Sophie looked him up and down as if she was measuring him for something. I thought I knew what it was, but as it turned out I was only half right and it was the other half that was most important.

Boris's eyes followed her as she went to sit beside Montrose who apologized for keeping us waiting.

'So can we start?' said Nell.

The prevailing mood was not sympathetic and I wasn't going to drop my poem into it. The timing was wrong, I had planned for my rendering to come last, the literary event (after all, it was the only one) of the evening.

I said we hadn't heard from Boris. Boris was waiting to hear from Sophie. Sophie was working on Montrose by a process of fermentation. According to *Chambers*, fermentation excites the emotions, it's an increase in biological activity, it compounds things already compounded. I go along with that. My grand-mother, my father's mother, used to make dandelion whisky, a cloudy yellow liquid like cabbage water. Brown froth ran down the necks of the bottles, smelling terrible and hissing. Grand-mother said that was the devil in it. The memory came back to me, including the smell, as I watched Sophie concentrating on Montrose. She was sitting quite still, no lock of hair escaping, no eyelids fluttering.

He was pinching up the crease in his trousers, I wondered if he wore golliwog stripes for fun or bravado. What I did know was that Sophie was getting through to Boris, though I didn't think she had purposed it. He was just side-effectual.

I hoped he would talk about his bones and tamp down the atmosphere and make it more receptive for my reading. But his biological activity is tied up with his work. He stood up, loomed. We weren't there to be loomed over, we were a group of friends with differing reactions and a broad spectrum of taste, you couldn't get much broader. I considered that with Montrose as artistic co-ordinator and me as emergent creator, we were more representative than any group of writers.

Sophie snapped her fingers at Boris. She probably intended to bring him out of his daze, but it was dismissive, a woman dismissing a man and the hopes and expectations she had aroused in him. To me it spoke, if not volumes at least one full-length novel which I might have written, given the time.

Boris picked up his Big Shopper and held it high. 'This is my salute to Art, my Celebration of the Word –' he was into upper cases, 'the Word for all seasons, this is my Euterpe.' He fished in the Big Shopper and brought out something wrapped in newspaper.

'Euwho?'

'The goddess of lyric poetry. I shall create her in stone to stand in the garden and proclaim this house a poets' house.'

'Sort of a logo,' Nell said.

'I shall make her taller than the trees.'

'You can't,' I said, 'it's against the law.'

'What law?'

'Ancient lights, to stop people building on top of the neigh-bours.'

120

'This is not a building!'

It was a clay figure of a woman. She was naked truth with nothing left out except the face which was a blob and could be anyone's. But the rope of hair with escaping tendrils, the curve of the neck and bosom and the odalisque pose were immediately recognizable. We all recognized it, even Montrose. His ears went back. I was shocked on Nell's behalf. I couldn't look at her. Sophie looked and laughed and put out her hand to Nell.

Boris was waiting, hungry for praise.

'She's lovely,' I said. 'So lifelike. Will you put all that detail into the stone?'

'I can cut stone to the fineness of a leaf.'

'I know. But in the garden we already have leaves.'

'You don't like my Euterpe!'

'I think she's gorgeous. I worry about what people will make of her when she's so much bigger. I don't think they'll think of poetry.'

Sophie, who should have kept quiet, said, 'Sweetie, that's what's needed. It'll bring writers in swarms.'

'Listen,' said Boris, 'I made a horse and because it had no genitals I am told it is not a real horse. I give this goddess the body of a woman and you say it is too much!'

'What if people like your statue for the wrong reasons?' said Montrose.

'I'd say that was a distinct possibility, wouldn't you?' Sophie smiled into his face with a lingering intimacy which I was sure couldn't exist. It was too soon.

But Boris believed it existed. His cheekbones went all Slav and Euterpe shook with emotion as he held her aloft. 'Look, look at her and tell me what are your wrong reasons!'

I said, 'It's in the eye of the beholder and we don't all have that kind of eye.'

'A true work of art does not need special eyes. The message is plain to all who look. If there is too little or too much there is not enough. Therefore this is without value!'

'You're too hard on yourself,' said Montrose.

'My husband is dedicated,' said Nell.

I said, 'I think it's a lovely idea. It will be part of the achievement of this Centre. Out there in the garden the first thing

121

people will see will be the word in stone. It's an honour for us all.' I thought what more does he want?

Maria said to Sophie, 'Guess you get most of the honour.'

Boris pulled Euterpe's head off.

I read my poem and they listened, all except Boris. He had gone, leaving the clay torso and the plastic carrier.

'What shall I do with it?' I said.

'Take it shopping,' said Nell.

When I picked up the model an awful thing happened. It broke in two. I had Sophie's torso in one hand and her legs in the other. I hadn't wanted to touch the thing anyway.

Montrose spoke to Sophie. 'I think it's yours.'

She pouted and bridled in a Regency-belle style. Nell said, 'I'll take it.'

Montrose signed to me that it was time for my reading. It was not a good time, but it had come.

I started too loudly:

> 'Music here falls softer
> Than blown roses on the grass. . . . '

I really blew those roses –

> 'This music on my senses lies
> Like tired eyelids on tired eyes –'

Reading on, I was caught up in the wonder of creation. Although it was my own creation I wondered at and venerated the words, chosen, each of them, like jewels for a crown.

> 'My heart is heavy in my breast
> It knows no joy, it knows no rest,
> And love is but a hollow jest.
> Is this my fate, this ceaseless toil
> Wasting my spirit and my powers,
> Squandering the precious hours
> In a drear and soulless moil –

When in the middle of the wood
The leaf is coaxed from out the bud
Grows green and gold all summer long,
One of a whispering forest throng,
Lives its allotted length of days
Then drifts a-down the autumn haze,
Nothing valued, nothing worth
To its rest in the fruitful earth?
If leaves and flowers fade away,
If thus they live and thus they die,
No blood, no tears and no dismay,
Here where the moss is cool and deep
And o'er the stream the willows weep
In death's embrace I choose to lie.'

I'd have liked a ripple of applause when I finished, a ripple
would have been enough, you don't clap hands for a lament. I
got a hush, they sat perfectly still, they could have been
stunned.

I gathered up my typescript. I hadn't needed to read, I had
the words by heart, *on* my heart, where my faith is, as my father
once said.

'Can we discuss it? The finer points – any points. I'm not
afraid of you saying what you think.'

Nell sighed. 'I think when you think you know what's coming
next it's real poetry.' I've always been able to depend on her
critical sense.

Sophie said, 'What's it called?'

' "Elegy".'

'Death's embrace is lovely,' said Nell.

I turned to Montrose. 'Did you like it?'

He nodded:

' "How sweet it were, with half-shut eyes to dream
    Like yonder light which lingers on the height. . . ." '

Sophie yawned, stretched, expanded, offering her beautiful
bosom to the air. Montrose turned in his chair to watch her.

123

'Very nice,' he said, and crossed his ankles. His ankle-bones shone pearly, either he wears very thin silk socks, or no socks at all. I notice details when I'm nervous.

Nell stood up, extending her hand to Sophie as to a child. Sophie took it and was led away. Like a child.

'Show's over.' Maria grinned and waved and followed them.

Montrose said, 'Your poem reminds me of someone. Tennyson.'

'He was an early influence.'

'That man had an easy life, never got into trouble or went hungry or ran off with a woman. I can't think why he wanted to lie on the beach and eat lotoses.'

'I expect it was poetic licence.'

'Remember how he goes on about Man being the boss but getting no rest? Forever climbing up the wave? Apples and flowers sit tight, he says, they toil not neither do they spin.'

'That wasn't him, that was the Bible – the lilies of the field.'

'Lord Alfred Tennyson wrote the "Song of the Lotos-Eaters" and you read it somewhere, maybe in school. "Music that gentlier on the spirit lies, Than tired eyelids on tired eyes." '

'*I* wrote that.'

' "How sweet it were, hearing the downward stream,
    With half-shut eyes ever to seem
    Falling asleep in a half-dream!
    To dream and dream, like yonder amber light,
    Which will not leave the myrrh-bush on the height."

Remember?'

'I remember what I wrote.'

'My guess is your teacher read it to the class and it stuck in the back of your mind.'

'That poem's mine, I wrote it, I was inspired to write it. Not Tennyson nor anyone else. Every word of it is mine!'

'What about "Propt on beds of amaranth and moly"? Moly's wild onion. His lordship must have been fond of onions, "The Lady of Shalott" is his too.'

If he thought he could take the edge off with a joke, let me down gently. . . . A knot of something was about to burst inside me. My voice shot up several bels, never mind decibels. 'I don't believe you! I've never heard of "The Lotos-Eaters"!'

'Miss Zeph, it's the easiest thing to pick up a simple rhyming pattern. Don't take my word, next time you're in the library check with the *Oxford Book of English Verse*.'

I rushed to the library in my lunch-break and there it was, page 845 of the *Oxford Book*: 'The Song of the Lotos-Eaters', by Alfred Lord Tennyson, all my best lines and a lot more which I wouldn't have written anyway.

With what joy I had received 'Music on my senses lies like tired eyelids on tired eyes'. . . . But where had I received it from? Suppose there are only so many systems of words and I'm hooked into Tennyson's system and will never be able to produce anything but reconstituted bits of his. . . .

I was in despair. Miss Abercorn's minus Ds used to put my back up. I mistrusted her judgement and took it gingerly when I took it at all. Montrose was another matter. He made me mistrust my inspiration.

I couldn't face going back to the office. I called from a phone box, using an assumed voice. 'I'm afraid Miss Pollock has had a mishap and won't be able to return to work this afternoon.' What sort of a mishap they wanted to know. 'I'm not at liberty to say,' I said. I'd think of something to say in the morning.

I found a football ground which was the emptiest place I could find. I'd lost my prime function and didn't want to be among people who still had theirs. I had no place in society and so far as Planet Earth was concerned I was just part of the re-cycling process.

I walked round and round that football pitch. The mud was ready for Saturday's game: gulls perching on the goal-posts turned their backs on me. Knowing how it felt to be an outcast wasn't going to enrich my writing. In future, whatever I experienced, in my mind or my skin, would stop there, I was never going to make a contribution to the sum of human knowledge.

Why had I thought I would? Who or what had given me that idea? Looking for someone to blame, I got to my father, telling me I could do anything if I had faith. Coming from him that was a joke. Coming to me, an impressionable child, it was criminal negligence. No wonder my mother was angry. She had tried to warn me. But there's no bug like the creative bug. It ate me alive, bones, juices and all.

I despised my father. Despite's an unproductive emotion, it fizzled a bit, then fizzled out. Anyway, I had no longer anything to produce. I was the husk known as Zephrine Pollock, a name which would appear only on the electoral roll.

Then I thought, perhaps he wasn't to blame, perhaps he was an instrument. Instrumentality – doing what he was told – he was good at. And if he hadn't been told, if it was a question of genetics, he wouldn't have had a choice.

But genesis would. Genesis would have a reason. I observed that the grass was marked out in white lines and half circles. It gave me a glimmer of hope. If genesis didn't have a reason, there'd be no football because no one would live long enough to work out the midfield, offside and goal areas. Or anything else for that matter. It would be chaos. There has to be a pattern and I got a rough idea what it is. I got it by looking at the way things are done, and undone, by people, and by nature who's always shifting plates, cutting up continents and blowing up islands. What I needed to know was where I came into it.

I walked round and round and the concept wound tighter and tighter and suddenly I saw the place in the pattern where I had always been. My place, ordained, decreed and destined for me. I had had a lapse of faith, that was all. I kicked an imaginary ball into goal and someone shouted from the grandstand.

'Decide?' said Maria. 'The money did that. I didn't have it so I didn't go.'

'Does he know?'

'Going to surprise him. Think he'll be pleased?'

I once saw my father surprised when his shoelace broke as he was tying it. He looked stupefied. 'Of course.'

'Got to find him first.'

'Haven't you got his address?'

'He said he'd write when he settled.'

'You mean you're going out there to search for him?' I just hope he wants to be found. 'Where did you get the money for the fare?'

'I sold my paintings.'

'You what?' I didn't mean to be rude, I was genuinely staggered. 'How? Who to?'

'A man saw my two pictures in the Charity Shop and asked if they had any more. They said no and it would be nice if he'd take those away.' Maria grinned. 'When I looked in to see if they'd been sold they gave me a phone number. I rang up and the man came round. I got everything out to show him and he bought the lot. Paid for my fare and a cup of coffee at the airport.'

'I'm glad for you.'

'He said they're ethnic art, a reaction against photo-realism.' Maria giggled. 'Could be he's got a lot of holes in his fence.'

'You must be very happy, having your work recognized and appreciated.'

'I'm happy for the money that's going to take me to my Edgar.'

Her Edgar. He belongs to her in so far as he belongs to anyone. But what's he doing in Jamaica? One answer is that he was happy there once. She has succeeded, her storms of paint and splinters have been understood and wanted. But it only matters to her because he matters. It's a question of relative values.

'What do you see in him?' I suppose I shouldn't have asked, even in the broad spectrum of enquiry.

'Love,' she said cheerfully. 'I see love. Maybe it's only mine, but I don't care, I have to have it.'

'You're wasting your time and money and your creative gift.'

'I've got plans for my creative gift. Going to make a baby for him.'

I was nauseated, my responses reduced to a digestive process. It took some swallowing, my father and a brown baby – my father, my mother, Maria and a brown baby.

'What's troubling you?' she said. 'Am I too black?' The idea of any baby, black or white, was nauseating. 'What troubles *me* is I don't see any love in you.'

My temper works like lemonade, fizzes up and runs over, makes bubbles. I treat it like lemonade and screw it up tight. 'There's more than one kind of love.'

'You telling me?'

127

'I love my work.'

'I'm talking about people, men and women. I never saw that kind of love in you.'

'I don't need it.'

'Honey, everyone needs it.'

'A writer isn't everyone.' Having said that, I saw that it was a half-truth, and saw the other half. A writer must be everyone, the halves must lock tight, but Maria wouldn't be able to put them together. 'What I feel is academic.'

'Got to be different, eh? That's how Crab got a dish on his back. He had nice eyes and pretty legs but he wanted to be different. He went to a wise woman and asked her to make him different. "Walk sideways," she said, "that will do nicely." But it wasn't enough for him, he pestered her to do something special. She got annoyed and threw a dish. It fell on his back and stuck. He never could get it off and he's still trying, that's why he runs sideways to this day.'

I suppose it was some sort of fable, to point a moral. 'I was born different. I don't know if that's good or bad, but I have to see it through.'

'What did Montrose say to you?'

'I don't want to talk about it.'

'Don't pay him too much mind. He's got big ideas, lovely for him, nothing for anyone else.'

'I shall have to advertise your room.'

'Last night wasn't the end of the world. You write what you think and it'll be great.' It was all I needed, Maria telling me how to write. 'There's something you should know, nothing to do with your writing. That child, Diggory, woke me in the middle of last night, shit-scared. I took him back to his bed and there was no one in the room, he'd been left alone.'

'Well?'

'So then he went to your Miss Sophie's door and cried like a puppy-dog. It's my opinion his mother was in there. What a thing, eh?'

'Thing?'

'Don't pretend you never knew anything like it before.'

'Why shouldn't Nell go and talk to Sophie if she wants to?'

When Maria rolls her eyes she does a thorough job. There's a split second when they're all whites and I'm afraid she won't be able to get her irises back.

Sunday morning I overslept and rose up in a panic thinking I was late for work. Flinging back my curtains I saw Dalton Toplady in the garden. I called, 'What are you doing?'

'Don't worry, I'll be careful where I tread.'

'You can walk on the weeds for all I care.'

'I like yellow daisies.' He put his arm round a clump and cuddled it. 'This is just how I want the garden of Beauty's palace to look.'

'That's ragwort. Briar roses would be more appropriate.'

'We'll be shooting in Stackpole Hall, the big house in the Park. The Park's too well kept for our story. But I can catch all the shots I need to illustrate a hundred years of neglect here in your back-yard. And the shed can be done over for the witch's gingerbread house.'

'Hansel and Gretel don't come into the Sleeping Beauty story.'

'They do if I say so.'

'I don't want pornography in my garden.'

'We'll be shooting the lake scene this morning. Come and watch.'

When I went down to the kitchen to make breakfast I smelled gas and called Boris to help check if there was a leak. Nell said four noses were better than one and they all came – Boris, Nell, Sophie and Diggory. Boris walked round sniffing. He spent so much time with the cooker, turning the taps on and off I thought he would gas us all.

'It's not in the pipes,' I said, 'it's in the air.'

Nell and Sophie had made a ring of their hands and caught Diggory between them, teasing him. He tried to escape, but they laughed and held him. He threw himself on his back on the floor, covered his face and screamed. When Nell tried to pick him up he reached out his arms for Sophie. She and Nell smiled at each other over his head.

'It is not in the air!' Boris seized a box of matches, struck

129

one and let it burn down to his fingers. There was a smell of scorched flesh. He looked terrible.

'We're filming this morning, we must go and make up.' Sophie scooped Diggory into her arms. 'I think honey-beige and eye-liner for him.'

'Diggory?'

'My leading man.' He locked his arms round her neck and she bore him away, singing that he was her sunshine, her only sunshine.

Boris blew on his fingers. 'Run cold water over your hand,' said Nell.

'Where are you going?'

'To church. I have one or two things to sort out.' She spoke lightly, I felt I'd missed a couple of sentences.

'She is not a believer,' Boris said when she'd gone. But I wouldn't put it past her to go through the motions. If I hear bells ringing for church I think oh, that's another thing. Perhaps she does too. 'This is a war-house,' said Boris.

'A what?'

'We have wars here, but no writers. It is not a writers' house.'

'Look,' I said, 'we have our differences but I'm a writer, this is my house, therefore it's a writer's house.'

'It is not an artist's house. I am not an artist. I thought God was using me. God, I thought, has put me on earth to cut stone and create such beauty as will turn people's thoughts away from themselves. When they see my work they will forget their lustfulness and sinfulness and think of the works of his hand.'

'Is that what you want?'

'Did he not shape man from the dust and carve woman from the man's rib? Did he not design fish in the sea and birds in the air and all creatures that run and creep on the earth?' He was beginning to look Old Testament as well as sound it. 'The work of the artist must reflect that of his Creator, there is no other source, all else is futile. You have seen the needles in a pine forest? Nothing can grow because of them.'

'So?'

'You look at my work, what do you see?'

130

'I thought your Euterpe was lovely. Just like – we all saw who she was like.'

'You did not see genesis.'

'Genesis?' Surprised and excited I cried, 'Genesis is at the bottom of every work of art!'

He held up his hand, pulpit-fashion. 'My work is like the pine-needles, barren, fit only for burning. I have allowed whispering voices to crowd out the one voice.'

I felt really sorry for him. I realized that he hadn't been talking about fights. The English language is full of silent letters, like the 'W' in whores.


Maria had caught sight of Sophie and Toplady with Diggory between them going across the park. 'What are they going to do with that child?'

'Shoot him, with a camera.'

'Will you let them put an innocent baby in a dirty picture?'

'If his mother doesn't object I don't see how I can.'

Maria's lip curled. 'Cat's a better mother than her. I'm going to watch out for him, someone's got to.'

Stackpole Hall is home to the local council. They moved in after it had been empty for years. They knocked down walls and took out some boisterous caryatids and installed a class system: the Mayor's parlour and council grandees have the ground floor, water and housing are on the first, health and welfare on the third, sewage and refuse in the basement.

The park has been updated. There are dog-toilets and a play area, functional swings and roundabouts – no prancing horses or coloured ropes, the kiddies sail through the air to the music of rusty iron. The lake still looks pretty with its blue-and-gold chocolate-wrappers floating on the surface. Paddling and swimming are forbidden, but local lads hold their noses and dive down to the old tyres on the bottom.

This Sunday morning Toplady had cordoned off one area and a boy was running to and fro to keep back spectators who were pressing on the rope.

I assured Maria that Diggory's father would be watching out for him. Boris was at the edge of the lake, looking across to where Sophie and the child were. She had Diggory by the hands and was swinging him round and round. We heard his delighted shrieks.

'She's going to make him sick,' said Maria. 'What are they up to?'

Toplady was unlashing a small boat from the roof rack of his car. 'Perhaps they're going to do a remake of *The African Queen*.'

Toplady saw me and beckoned. 'Come and untie this knot so we can get this thing down.'

'What for?'

'You've got nimbler fingers than me.'

'Why the boat?'

'We're shooting the mother-love scene. It's one of the human touches which will make this four-star viewing, five, if Sophie gets it right.'

I teased the knot loose and we got the boat off the car. It was a fibre-glass job, quite light. I said, 'Sophie's got to get into this?'

'Her and the kid.'

'Not Diggory!'

'She's playing his mother, she takes him on the lake with the idea of drowning him, but when it comes to the crunch she can't do it.'

'Is this Red Riding Hood or Snow White?'

'It's an adaptation of Cinderella.'

'Cinderella didn't have a child. At least not until after the glass slipper bit.'

'We've dispensed with the slipper. The story hinges on the Ugly Sisters trying to get into Sinella's bra. A great scene, hilarious, guaranteed to turn them on.'

'What about Prince Charming?'

'He's a Middle East Shake with a shakedom full of oil. If Sinella plays her cards right he'll add her to his harem. But she must be a virgin. Help me get the boat to the water.'

'You can't put Diggory in that!'

'He'll come to no harm. She takes him to the lake because the Shake mustn't know she's slept around. She's got to destroy the evidence. But mother-love gets the better of her, we'll have shots of her clasping the kid to her bosom and close-ups of her weeping.

Sophie doesn't need technical assistance, she's a natural, presses the button and down come the tears.'

'Does Diggory's mother know you're going to use him?'

'Lift your end, you'll have me in the mud.'

'*Does* she?'

'I haven't signed him up, if that's what you mean.'

'Have you asked his father?' But he shouted to the boy at the rope to come and launch the boat. As soon as the boy moved away, some spectators ducked under the cordon. Toplady roared, 'Nigel! Keep those creeps out!'

Nigel was a skinhead, he had a black plastic bolero and arms tattooed green. I was too far away to make out the design. He ran at the spectators and clapped the clapper-board in their faces.

'Hey, you!' Toplady called to Boris. 'Give us a hand!'

Boris, his arms folded in a magisterial pose, did not look round. He was watching a man with a camcorder on his shoulder prowling round Sophie, occasionally sinking to his knees as if in prayer. Another man was setting up microphones wired to a van labelled 'Video-services'.

'I didn't realize it was such a business,' I said. 'Personally I find creativity wholly private –'

'Help me launch this thing.'

'Can't someone else do it?'

'They're busy.'

'I don't want to get into the mud.'

'Listen,' each pock in Toplady's nose deepened and darkened, 'this gear is hired, do I have to tell you it costs an arm and a leg? Every minute we're not shooting is money down the drain. Get her round! Didn't you ever push a boat out before? You don't launch it on its beam, for Chrissakes!'

I yelled 'Don't push!' but too late. The boat dropped into the water and sent back wavelets which I wasn't quick enough to dodge. Water coming into my shoes gives me angst. My mother maintained that wet feet are the greatest health hazard: if you don't get pneumonia and die, you lay the foundation for haemorrhoids. 'I'm soaked!'

Toplady was holding on to the boat, his feet well clear of the water. He ordered me to stand aside. 'Let them come aboard.'

133

He signalled to Sophie. She wasn't keen. She called was it safe? 'It's the technological alternative to walking on the water.' He picked Diggory up and dropped him in the boat. The boat rocked, Diggory wept, put up his arms to Sophie.

'Hold it! Fine! Keep him looking like that and we'll have a blue weepie.'

'That child's not play-acting,' said Maria, coming to the water's edge. 'Can't you see he's sick?'

'If he is, the sooner we get this taped the better.' Toplady hustled Sophie into the boat. 'I want you over there by the willow.'

'I can't row!'

'You don't need to. There's a cross-current, you'll drift. Keep the kid soulful and be ready to start your action when I say.'

He gave the boat a shove, it spun round and round, Sophie clinging to the sides, Diggory in the bottom. 'Ready to run!' shouted Toplady to the man with the camera. 'Are you hooked up, Fred?'

The man with the microphones called back, 'Get the kid to scream, I'm testing for level.'

Maria said, 'Didn't nobody ever tell these people about themselves?'

Toplady was ready. He lit a thin cigar, the Hollywood touch. 'Tomorrow we do the ballroom scene. It's the Council's day off, they've given us *carte blanche*, so long as we leave everything as we find it. All we have to do is shift the chairs and put up some drapes.'

'You know they've done the whole place over in mushroom gloss?' I said. 'How will that look on film?'

'It'll make a nice contrast to the costumes. When Sinella runs down the grand staircase doing her striptease we'll highlight her focal points – lipstick, blusher and glitter dust will bring them right out of the home screen. Geoff! See you keep that bloody litter-bin out of shot.'

'Maybe it will rain.' Maria sounded hopeful.

'No problem. We can shoot in low light, dawn to dusk in fact.'

Fred, with the mikes, said he was picking up crisp-crunching from the spectators.

'Why the lake?' I said. 'How is that relevant?'

134

'I bring in water whenever I can. It concentrates the action.'

'There's no water in Cinderella.'

'You think we could run for an hour on kitchen-sink and ballroom scenes? This is a composite, it takes in some other old stuff.'

'What stuff?'

'Hansel and Gretel, the Sleeping Beauty. We'll shine a light into the depths of human nature. It's all there, you know, cannibalism, girls turned on by monsters and sleeping with toads.'

The boat, rocking gently as a cradle, was drifting towards the willow on the far bank. Sophie now seemed to be enjoying herself, leaning over the side and fluffing up water to encourage Diggory.

Toplady cupped his hands round his mouth and shouted at the spectators. 'Hush up, you buggers! We're going to go – No, hold it! That bloody litter-bin's in the frame.' Everything waited, except the boat which was twirling prettily and self-consciously in the middle of the lake. 'Somebody move it! Hide it!'

There it was, a clone of the bin that had killed my mother, park-green metal with a black plastic liner to facilitate easy emptying. Nigel, the skinhead, sprang at it and tried to wrench it off its base. It was set into concrete and he lost his grip and fell on his bottom. The spectators laughed. One ducked under the cordon, broke a trailing branch from the willow and draped it over the bin. The rest cheered.

'For Chrissakes, let's get on,' said Toplady without a word of appreciation.

It made quite a picture: the bright blue boat, sun on the water, Sophie wearing a breakfront dress, her hair unbound and falling over her shoulders in a golden shower. Fairy-tale, you could say. Boris groaned on a deep Slav note. Maria said, 'Sweet-voiced crocodile going to love her.' Toplady shouted, 'Geoff, start rolling! AAAAAND – ACTION!'

Sophie was wonderful. She rocked Diggory in her arms, smiling radiantly into the camera, pure Mothercare. Then she raised Diggory aloft. Her hands were under his armpits, she

135

gazed up at him, head back, revealing the line of her lovely throat, the classic maternal adoration pose.

'Darlings, that's great,' breathed Toplady, and fervently kissed his cigar. For the moment he loved us all.

Then the situation changed. From Diggory's point of view it must have been in urgent need of changing. He was suspended in mid-air over an expanse of water, he may have loved Sophie but he knew nothing about acting. He panicked, squirmed and lashed out with arms and legs. Sophie held on, Diggory kicked her in the face, the boat bobbed like a cork. He might have dropped without much damage into the bottom, but he seemed to project himself with his arms and legs. He hit the water with a mighty splash. No one moved. He went down, leaving a skin of smooth water, even the ripples stood still. We were all in shock.

I don't know what thoughts flashed through that child's brain while he was drowning, but I did some thinking myself. I thought of Nell in church, praying when she should be here taking care of her child: I thought, this is his first time down, he's got two more to go, what will it do to him, swallowing dirty water? I thought, I don't put it past Toplady to have intended it, he and Sophie could have engineered this to get extra titillation into the movie.

A dog strolled out and sniffed the camouflaged litter-bin and that was a signal for the shock to become corporate reaction. The rope cordon was swept aside, the spectators rushed to the water's edge. Men shouted, women screamed, a concerted howl went up when Diggory surfaced, floating in his pink nylon playsuit. He was face-down, arms outstretched, heels just showing above the surface of the water.

A woman cried, 'He's dead!'

Sophie leaned over the side of the boat, beat the water with her hands, trying to get to him. She kept crying that she couldn't swim. Nor can I, but I went in over my ankles hoping to encourage someone who could. A man on the other bank started taking off his shoes, Sophie bounced around screaming for someone to do something. The boat stood on end, she lost her balance, fell backwards and rocked away down-lake with her head and shoulders in the bottom out of sight and her knees draped over the side. Diggory continued to float like a water-logged flower.

I looked round for Boris. He was watching the scene, apparently unmoved. I couldn't believe it. I cried, 'Boris – help him!'

I don't think he heard, I don't think anyone did. There was general pandemonium, an elderly man waded in up to his waist, trod on something on the bottom and went under. His hat floated helpfully in Diggory's direction. A shrill roar went up, people were throwing off coats, the man who owned the dog was seen urging it to the rescue. The dog went to the edge and obligingly lapped a little water.

Then something rushed past with the fizz and speed of a rocket. The lake split open as Maria dived in. She struck out, arm over arm, feet churning, raising a storm of water in her wake. It overtook the luckless man who had just come up for the first time, and went on to slop over the feet of those on the bank. Someone waded in far enough to give the man a hand and pull him out. The spectators cheered, but fell silent as Maria reached Diggory. Our assembled breaths were held when she turned him on his back.

He can be relied on to bite the hand that feeds, or helps, him. As soon as his face was clear of the water he thrashed wildly, trying to break Maria's hold. He was so obviously alive a glad chorus went up from people on the bank. But it was as much as Maria could do to get him ashore. I went to help her over the last stretch of mud, so did Fred, the sound man. Toplady waited, hands on hips, looking exasperated. Boris had not stirred from his magisterial pose.

Maria and I got Diggory ashore between us. There was no need for resuscitation, he was fighting mad, any attempt to give him the kiss of life would have given the kisser a black eye.

'You were wonderful!' I told Maria.

She dashed a string of weed off her cheek. 'First time I ever swam in cabbage soup.'

I put my coat round them both and we ran home across the park. First priority was to plunge Diggory into a hot bath and get him into dry clothes. We left him penned in his cot, furiously shaking the bars, while Maria changed and I went to make hot drinks.

Toplady arrived as the milk was coming to the boil. 'Is the kid okay?'

'No thanks to you,' I said, whipping the saucepan aside.

'You shouldn't boil milk for coffee. In point of fact, that little episode adds up to a great sequence. We kept the camera running and I'll work it into the storyline.'

'You didn't even ask Diggory's mother if you could put him in the film –'

'Every mother wants her baby to be another Shirley Temple. I must say he played up like part of the talent.' He put out a hand to the cups. 'I don't take milk in coffee.'

I struck his hand aside. 'This isn't for you, the milk's for Diggory and the coffee's for Maria.'

He shrugged. 'I guess that wraps up the day's shooting. I'll be in touch about fixing your shed for the gingerbread house.'

'Where's Sophie?'

'Signing autographs.'

I carried the drinks upstairs. Maria was sitting with Diggory. He had quietened and was tugging her hair through the bars of his cot. 'Why do you let him do that?'

'Don't you realize he's got to keep in touch? He's scared we'll go away some place where we belong and he doesn't.'

'That's no reason to let him hurt you.'

'This child couldn't hurt me. What hurts me is seeing him lonely, nobody caring that he's no place to go. He crawls under beds and into corners to hide. How's he ever going to stand up like a man?'

'He's got parents –'

'Who dey?'

'Just because you and Nell don't see eye to eye –'

'When I look in her eye I see a jumby.'

'A what?'

'A bad spirit.'

'You should take to writing, there's a market for the paranormal.'

138

'She's going to destroy that white doll.'

'If you're talking about her and Sophie you're over-reacting again. Because you don't feel the way they do doesn't make it diabolic.' She removed one of her dreadlocks from Diggory's grasp and lifted him out of his cot. 'Where are you taking him?'

'To my bed and tell him a nice story.'

I was warming my feet in the oven when Nell returned. 'How was the service?'

'What service? You'll give yourself chilblains.'

'You missed the filming. Diggory fell in the lake.'

'What?'

'Maria got him out. She was the only one not afraid of the yuck.'

'Where is he?'

'It's all right, we've bathed him and changed his clothes.' She turned to go upstairs. 'He's okay, Maria's taking care of him.'

'What happened?'

'They were shooting a big scene, Sinella and her child in a boat.'

'Sinella?'

'Sophie plays the part. I knew you'd be worried.'

'Of course I'm worried!' She was halfway along the passage when Boris came in the front door. I heard her cry, 'Where have *you* been?'

I didn't hear his reply. I heard her crying, 'You were there? And just watched? You can swim, you swim like a fish, but you would have let him drown!'

Boris said, 'Fish don't swim in that water.'

'You did nothing? You didn't try to save him? Your own child?'

'He is not my child.'

He spoke so quietly I couldn't be sure I'd heard him say that, it could have been a pre-cognitive echo in my mind of what he might say. I knew Diggory wasn't his. Although I would never betray Nell's confidence I did think it would have been better

139

for them both if Boris knew the truth. I went and looked along the passage.

He was in the open door with his back to the light. Nell was facing him and I couldn't see her face.

She said, 'What do you mean?' It was all she could say, it's what you say when you know what's meant, and the implications.

'I have always known you are deceiving me.'

By putting it in the present tense I hoped he might mean to make it pardonable, hint that he was prepared to forgive her and keep it between their two selves. But put that way it was also pretty insulting, implied that he hadn't been bothered. It took Nell down a permanent peg, and gave him a private standing joke. Knowing their two selves as she did, she must be thinking how often he must have enjoyed the laugh.

'You bastard,' she said, and went upstairs.

It doesn't have to be a 'book', there are other names. They don't all mean literature. I rather fancy fascicle, which means a bundle, a part of a book which is being issued in parts. Like Dickens. Or variorum, which means a succession of changes (jocular). I do think some humour is essential. Or there's bio-data. Biographical information is the stuff of every novel. I think I like meta-fiction best, it means above and beyond fiction, something more than a story.

My publishers won't have to pay anyone to design the dust-jacket, it materialized while I was watching a TV commercial about a caring bank. I saw it opened out like the wings of a bird, 'Zephrine Pollock – a Meta-Fiction', the background scarlet, the letters black and plain as a newspaper headline. A bookstall is a cut-throat place: a serious work must first catch the eye, then the mind. On the back flap my photograph is slightly fuzzy, like the photographs of spirit manifestations. I'm shown deep in thought, those thoughts which I have expressed in page after page of limpid prose. The blurb says I achieve a powerful evocation of the human condition, encompassing the whole range of human emotions, at once compassionate and compelling, stark realism mingled with subtle yet arresting nuances. 'A major writer is born.'

140

I don't subscribe to Boris's idea of one work, one life – I can't afford to. There are books queuing up in me to be written. They are the glomeration of facts, however simple. I see now how simple they are: look at the one that there are booklice that eat books, and a book spider that eats the lice. It goes straight back to Genesis.

I've been reading the Book of because the question of language is still paramount. Mine will be pure – I don't mean pious or innocent or healthy. I mean unmixed, whole.

Genesis may be the first book, but it treats everything as read. God named a few things as he went along: day and night and earth and sea and the sky which he called Heaven. Only four rivers are identified and the only one that sounds familiar is the Euphrates. It was left to Adam to name the animals and birds. I'd like to know how he came by words like chimpanzee, hippopotamus, budgerigar and pterodactyl. Woman, of course, is derivative.

So far as I can see, all Adam and Eve learned from the Tree of Knowledge was the fact that they had no clothes, which led them to make fig-leaf aprons. But fig-leaves weren't enough, they had to have fur coats and that's where it started to go wrong. I stop there: I'm into the birth of human nature only in so far as it relates to the birth of language and I'm not going to get any help from the Book of Genesis.

Montrose is right when he says literature is what we do best. But we've let the English language run riot. Three-quarters of the words in the dictionary are never used: who needs bellibone, probouleutic, procacity, smaragd, theow, zumbooruk, zelotypia or ladycow, to name but a few? What's wanted is narrative prose which is absolutely true. It has to be dug out from under the old Norse and Eurospeak. No more words of a lie.

Vocabulary is a jungle, a teeming mass of words, the living and the dead, obsolete and archaic all mixed together. But it was elemental once, before Adam's. I borrowed a book from the library about the birth of language. There were pages on Darwin and Plato and about how Man made up the names of animals out of raw sounds. Chimpanzee and budgerigar were never that raw.

141

★

Maria came to tell me that her papers were through and she was leaving.

'You don't even know where he is.'

'He sent me a nice picture of Montego Bay. I don't have to know where he's living, I know him.'

She was bright-eyed and bushy-tailed. It's called love, I wouldn't want anyone to feel so sure of me. 'What does Montrose say about you going?'

'None of his business. You can tell him I've gone after I've gone, the longer after the better.'

'Why?'

'Better for you. Let him go on paying rent for me, and tell him when you've rented the room to somebody else.'

'I couldn't do that.'

'You could, you need the money.'

'Would he stop you going?'

'Let him try!'

I went with her to Gatwick. We had coffee while we waited for her flight to be called. I paid. She wouldn't say how much money she had. I think it was very little. 'You're wrong not to tell Montrose, he'd like to be here to see you off. He'll be hurt.'

She was looking about her, a-glitter with excitement. 'I was never on an aeroplane before!'

'It's no different from being on a bus, except that you only see clouds through the window.'

'Can't wait to be up there with them!'

I said, 'Coffee this early turns my stomach.'

'What am I to tell Edgar about you? He wrote all over that picture postcard, how is she, what's she doing, is she happy, has she published her book?'

'Tell him yes.'

When her flight was indicated she thought it wouldn't wait, like catching a bus she'd have to run for it. She hung round my neck, I think she cried, her face was wet. She kissed me and was away, her beadwork bag bucking on her hip.

I expect to see her again. She'll find him on the island and he won't be able to lose her. If he comes back to this

142

country so will she. If there's no market for her pictures in Jamaica she'll find some way to raise the fare. She'll cut sugar-cane.

I arrived home to find Nell and Toplady in the garden. I tried to duck out of sight, but Nell saw me and beckoned. Toplady had his arm round her neck, his hand over her breast.

He made an attempt to get his other arm round me. I side-stepped and snagged my tights on a dead Christmas tree.

'We could use that,' he said, 'as a symbol for our time.'

'A symbol of what?' said Nell.

'Acid rain.'

'Does this film have to be completely foul?'

'I'd be a total wally as a director if it was. There'll be moments of rare beauty and pathos – like when you weep for the starving children.'

'What starving children?'

'You're fattening them for the oven, remember? They're shut up in the gingerbread house, eating it from inside out. You tell them to stick their arms out of the window so you can see how they're shaping, and the little beggars push out a broomstick. Being short-sighted, it moves you to tears.'

'You?' I said to Nell.

'She's playing the witch in the Hansel and Gretel sequence. Pretty and young, but myopic. She runs a café which is not doing well and she wants to try some new fillings. Babyburgers.'

'That's horrible!'

'It was written for kids, it won't upset adults.'

'Rather fun,' said Nell. His thumb was running round inside the neck of her dress. She smiled, including me.

'We'll have to re-position the shed, shift it so as to get the window. We'll nail on polystyrene strips, paint them pink and yellow, put sellotape criss-cross over the window to look like it's diamond panes and a twist of plastic to make a sugar chimney. It will look good enough to eat when we've finished.'

'Gingerbread is dark brown,' I said.

'Can't have that, it would come over looking like wood. I'd like to be contemporary and make it a burger house, but it

143

would cost, shaping and sticking on separate buns. It will be more of a Battenburger. Working on a shoestring you're bound to lose some of the finer points.'

'This shed has literary associations. I wrote my first stories in it.'

'Be worth a free tape and publicity to you.'

'Publicity?'

'I'll put it in the credits. When people see my movie they'll pay to come and live here.'

'I don't want those sort of people!'

Toplady squeezed Nell's neck. 'Take you to dinner?'

'That would be lovely.'

'We'll discuss your big scene.' To me, he said, 'Don't worry, we'll strip off the polystyrene and put in some latex cobwebs to make up for any we knock down. You'll never know we were here.'

'Look –'

'I've looked. This place inspires me. I create out of what I lack, not what I have.'

'It's the principle I object to.'

'What principle?' said Nell.

Toplady turned and went. Watching him tread the cow-parsnip made me bitter. 'You're my oldest friend,' I said to her, 'but I've never been close to you. He's closer than I am.'

'He suits me at this point in time.'

'Is that because of Sophie?'

She looked at me and laughed. ' "Colour stained her cheeks". Zeph, you'll never get anywhere if you don't loosen up.'

'Loosening up has been my primary concern, as a writer I am fully liberated.'

'That was a lovely poem you read to us, about moonlight and roses.'

'Roses and death. It was an exercise, I was trying out a technique. I have to have a different one for everything I write. The substance decides the treatment.'

'You've got bags of technique. You always had. Remember how it vexed Miss Abercorn?'

'She didn't approve of *Ulysses*.'

144

'Mood stuff's fine, yours could make the seminars at Berkeley. But you need a stiff injection of the real thing if you're going to get on the best-seller lists.'

'What real thing?'

'Life.'

'Thanks,' I said, feeling colour stain my cheeks, and elsewhere. 'I'd forgotten about life, I'll try to bring it in.'

'Zeph, you'll go to the top of the ratings, way above Krantz and le Carré.'

'I shan't write like anyone else, I'll be unique, exclusive to myself. With me it's physical as well as mental, I feel it in my veins.'

'You mean it's your blood-group?'

'My blood-group's the same as billions of other people's, my creative identity is my own, it will take over when it's ready. No use trying to force it, I have to wait, prepare myself to *be* myself – I can only be that when I'm writing. A still small voice speaks and tells me what to write. All I have to do is put in the commas.'

'Where does the voice come from?'

'From my corpuscles. Where else?'

Irony was lost on her. She was doing my thing with a strand of rye-grass: will, won't, this year, next year, sometime. She looked up. 'There's been a slight change of plan. Boris has moved into Sophie's room and she's come in with me. So far as you're concerned, the financial situation's unchanged.'

'Other things are changed.'

'Yes, that shook me too. Imagine, wife and mother and never knew I had this side to my nature. Hallelujah, I'm a dyke.'

'A what?'

'A lesbian, if you prefer it.'

'I don't.'

'It's a liberal sort of word, relates to horny old fishermen and big Greek mommas and newborn babies – anyone who happens to live on Lesbos.'

'It's over-related. Relative to what *you* mean by it, it's unnatural.'

'What Sophie and I have is a variation on a basic theme, even you can't call sex unnatural.'

145

'I think it's over-rated.'

'Come off it, you're living your old age first. Relax, find someone to show you a good time.'

'My good time will be writing my books and I shan't need anyone to show me.'

She licked her fingers and ran them up her front hair, frizzing it. 'It'll be a lot of fun going on films. Something different, anyway.'

'I can see you're into difference!'

'Are you going out tonight?'

'Why?'

'Be an angel and keep an ear open for Diggy. You'll be the only one home, Sophie's gone for a massage.'

'Can't Boris keep an ear open?'

'He's incommunicado, locked himself in and put his shoes outside the door.'

'To be cleaned?'

'To show he's there and not talking.'

'He hates me.'

'Boris does?'

'Diggory.'

'You're wrong. Diggy's the world's little sweetheart, loves everyone. He won't be any trouble. When I've put him down he'll sleep the clock round.'

'You've left him alone before, why are you fussing now?'

'He was nearly drowned, remember?' She frowned up into her frizz. 'It takes something like that to make you realize how much your child means to you.'

If she was using the second-person pronoun to give me a share of motherhood it wasn't working. I said, 'I expect to go out myself.'

'Somewhere special?'

'To meet a critic.'

'What's he going to crit?'

'Look, I can't be responsible for Diggory. I don't know the first thing about babies. He might get nappy-rash and I'd be useless.'

She laughed. 'Idiot. No matter, I'll be back early. It won't be a deprivation. The movie mogul's idea of supper is probably a sesame bun at McDonald's.'

146

I convinced myself that I ought to go and see Montrose to break the news of Maria's departure: a letter would be too formal, a phone-call too casual. Besides, it may or may not be true that I don't need anyone to show me my good time. There are times when I can do with a push in a direction. Any direction.

Cousin Gladys no longer lives in that street. Her house has been done over shrimp-pink and the new owners have a Volvo in the front garden. Gladys has either died or gone into an old people's home. Wherever she is, they'll know they've got her. I think of her egging my mother on – why is an egg thought to be urgent? The dictionary says it's from Old Norse meaning edge.

They come out of the brickwork when I go back there: my mother, Gladys, Maria and my father. All along the street I walk through their routines, their bitching and conspiring, and my father percolating. My heightened sensibilities are at an all-time high.

Re-entering that house is a dispiriting experience. The same strings are on the doormat where it has worn through to the canvas. Along the passage I put my fingers into the crack in the wall and dislodge a similar shower of plaster.

I went upstairs and knocked on Montrose's door. When he opened, he frowned, I was probably interrupting something.

'Miss Zeph. Come in.'

I said, 'Maria's gone.'

'Gone where?'

'To Jamaica. To my father.'

'Will you take coffee? I'm afraid I have no facilities for anything more.' He poured water from a kettle which showed no sign of boiling or having recently boiled. Bad cooking must run in the family. I thought Jamaican coffee was supposed to be good, but his tasted muddy. I've played enough netball to know how mud tastes.

'What did she use for the fare?'

'She sold her pictures.'

'She did!' It wasn't a question, it was a bravo.

'She found someone who liked them because they're a reaction against photo-realism.' He nodded, looking at his table

147

which was covered with open books. I had interrupted something. 'I thought you'd want to know about her going.'

'I'm happy for her. And for him. He's lost without her.'

'Lost is his natural condition.'

'Do you know why he went to Jamaica?'

'He had a nice time there once.' I hadn't come to talk about him. I picked up one of the books. '*Beowulf*?'

'I like monsters.'

'I'm into the birth of language. Darwin and Plato,' I said to show the level I was on. 'And Kant – Emmanuel.' He sat down, facing me. 'Language is the instrument of human reason. People couldn't think before they had words. They couldn't make up their minds, they didn't have minds.' Maria gives everything away through her skin, she glitters for anger and joy, sparkles for fun. His reveals nothing, it makes him very private. 'Come to think of it, words are our only creation, everything else was there already.'

'You're talking about your novel?'

'I'm talking about narrative style. The Genesis version. According to Genesis, Adam named the animals. If he did it in basic Hebrew, where does basic English come in?'

'Words come from all over. They're still coming.'

'What I'm asking is – dog, cat, bird and thing are all O.E. in *Chambers*. But are they basic? Are they pure?'

'Maybe you should leave your dictionary alone for a while.'

'Look,' I said, 'you practically destroyed me with that business about Lotos-Eaters. But you failed to take into account the all-important fact that truth can only be expressed in certain terms. Tennyson got in before me because he was born before me. I come to write about the self-same things, music and roses and death, and naturally I pick some of the same words, they happen to be the definitive ones. People think Bacon wrote Shakespeare because he used the same words.'

'Your choice was excellent.'

'I shan't write any more poetry. It was a mistake, more of a deliberate delusion. I see that now. I wasn't going far enough, I made myself a prisoner of my limitations – and Tennyson's,

148

and everyone's who accepts words at their current face value. Words have degenerated. I shall strip off the inexactitudes, cut out adverbials and modifiers. Analogies, likening one thing to another for the sake of effect is falsifying. I am aiming at crystal clarity.'

'What will you write about?'

'Everything.'

'Not everything can be put into words.'

'You're doing English Literature, so tell me what's missing. Who misses most? Somerset Maugham or *Beowulf*? I'm talking about techniques.'

'All methods are good if you have talent.'

'You think I don't have?'

'I think you will surprise us.'

'Some writers plunge straight in and rely on making a big splash. I have to achieve individuality.'

'Like Miss Ivy Compton-Burnett?'

'Like nobody.'

'You should talk to an etymologist.'

'I'm not interested in insects.' He smiled, widely for him, showing his canines which are white and almond-shaped. 'I shall learn from my mistakes, but I haven't time to make any more.'

'Someone said, in big things even to have wished is enough.'

He's doing English literature. I'm on my own. Taking my problem to him was another mistake. It had better be the last. Non-writers don't understand writers, writers don't even understand other writers.

I thought of Orange, working her way through four-letter words. She could be into double figures by now. That's not technique, it's martyrdom.

I thought someone had the radio on extra loud. I could hear it through the closed front door. Pop the Communicator gets to everyone with blood-thumps and caterwauling, attempts at articulation.

But when I got inside the house it wasn't radio, it was actual. Someone was wailing and thumping upstairs. I guessed who, my neck-hairs pricked.

149

He was outside Sophie's room which is now Boris's. He had one of Boris's shoes and was hitting the door again and again with a rhythm as if he'd been at it for hours. He was howling like a dog.

It got to me, the sound and sight of him making a wailing wall of one of my bedroom doors. I shouted, 'Stoppit!' He pitched his voice higher. I seized him by the slack of his sleeping-suit. It's too big for him, he twisted inside it and finished up facing me. He had howled like a dog, now he hissed like a cat and his eyes were tawny like a cat's.

It doesn't matter how old he is, he's all there already. Looking at him I get a pretty good idea what he's going to be. A cold-hearted macho.

I didn't prolong the look, but as I yanked him up, a sort of trapdoor opened in the seat of his sleeping-suit and revealed his skinny bottom. All his ingredients are there, but as yet they're in short supply.

'What on earth are you doing?' It was pointless because I knew what he was doing and I knew he wouldn't tell me anyway. He aimed a blow at me with Boris's shoe which was shaped to Boris's bunion.

The only way to hold him was on my hip, pinioned under my left arm. With my free hand I hammered on Sophie's door.

'Boris, are you there?' The door, of course, was locked. I rattled the knob. 'Boris, open up!' I didn't even know if he was inside, the shoes proved nothing, he must have had more than one pair. 'Diggory wants you. . . .' That was untrue, Diggory would be wanting Sophie. 'Look, he's in a state and I don't know what to do. Please help. . . .'

Diggory jack-knifed and hammered my calf with both his feet. His feet are like iron.

'Boris, for God's sake . . . .' If he wasn't there, *I* was wailing at the wall.

Diggory broke into the blood-curdling yells his sort make in supermarkets when they're dragged past the chocolate Rollos.

I let him slip to the floor and ran downstairs. I'll never be able to write until I'm free of domestic realism. I can't see Iris writing *The Sea, The Sea* in an atmosphere of domestic realism.

150

Whoever said, in big things to have wished is enough, was a wimp.

The domestic realism was following me, flop, flop on every stair. I thought, if I don't look round he'll go somewhere else. I went into the kitchen and slammed the door.

That was the signal for cries pumped out as he hauled himself along the passage. When he reached the kitchen door he drummed on it with his fists. I shouted to him to go away, but the door-handle turned and there he was, upright in the door-way.

He was trembling with effort but he was totally self-supporting, not holding on to anything.

'Bravo!' It might be the first time he'd done it, an achievement.

He dropped on all fours and came at me, intent on vengeance. He made for my ankle and would have bitten it if I hadn't hauled myself on to the kitchen table. I could feel a packet of cornflakes pulverizing under me. I couldn't stay, it was too ridiculous. I hopped off on the other side. 'Damn you!' I spoke to Nell and Toplady, but Diggory knew the word and thought I meant it for him. He crouched on the floor, glaring, his lips moved, moistened. Nell says it's not that he can't talk, he will when he's ready to articulate fully.

'Why don't I tuck you up in bed?' I said. 'It's draughty on the floor and Mummy' – calling Nell that was part of the absurdity – 'will expect you to be asleep when she comes home. Which will be any minute now.' Any of the next one hundred and eighty or so minutes, I said under my breath.

I held his gaze and he held mine. I don't know which of us held tightest, but there was no communication. I moved towards him, slowly and cautiously. When I was close, I held out my arms, putting up my thumbs in a playful parental sort of way. He gave me a stone-dead stare and scuttled under the sink.

'You'd better not stay there, the waste-pipe leaks.' He opened the pedal-bin and threw out some banana-skins. 'And there are spiders as big as your head.' That seemed to register a flicker of something, interest, or scorn. He dug deeper into the bin and dragged out potato-peelings.

151

'You little tyke!' I caught his feet, pulled him and the bin from under the sink. He clutched the bin to him. I had to turn him upside down to dislodge it. I've seen Nell carry him by his feet as if he's a thing. But he's *her* thing, I'm not entitled to do it.

The only way I could stop him getting his teeth into my leg was by kneeing him in the face. He fought me on every stair to Nell's door. By the time I'd dumped him in his cot and dragged up the side to keep him in, I was shagged out.

He wasn't, he wrenched at the bars and the cot-side would have fallen if I hadn't held on to it.

He played another card, stood up in his cot facing me, motionless. I thought it was all over and I'd won. 'Good boy.'

His eyes rounded into bubbles, his nostrils flared, his mouth snapped shut, his ribs arched. He drew a breath, and held it.

Ordinarily he's a skinny child which is not to be wondered at the way he's always putting himself about. But a skinful of air didn't seem to fatten him, he just turned damask red – the fabric, not the rose. A vein sprang up his neck, his jugular, I thought, starting to worry. All I know about small children is that they mustn't be allowed to put their heads into plastic bags.

The rabbits on his sleeping-suit trembled under the strain, he himself was rigid. He was quite capable of suffocating without any artificial aid.

'You realize I could bust you.' I clapped my hands together. 'Of course it would make an awful mess – if you bust a paper bag it splits.'

His cheeks were tight as apples and there was an adult frown of pain between his eyes. I thought, if he loses consciousness he'll have to lose his breath. I felt sorry for so much wasted effort.

'There's a story about a wolf that huffed and puffed and blew a house down. But it was a straw house and when he tried to do the same to a brick house he blew himself up.'

I had to hand it to him, he kept his dignity, released the merest whistle from between closed lips.

'Sit down,' I said, 'and I'll tell you the story of the three bears: Father Bear, Mamma Bear and Baby Bear. And a little

152

girl called Goldilocks. One day she was walking in the woods, and she found a pretty house. She knocked, but no one was home, so she went in and looked around. Know what she saw? Three chairs: a very big one, a not so big one, and a very little one. And on the table were three bowls: a very big bowl, a not so big bowl, and a little bowl. The very big bowl was Father Bear's, the not so big bowl was Mamma Bear's, and the littlest bowl was Baby Bear's.'

Children don't learn from repetition. A dog might, if you keep hitting it on the nose it may come to associate the blow with whatever it's doing and stop doing it.

Releasing the last of his breath Diggory uttered the one word: 'Nancy.'

'The little girl's name was Goldilocks.' I enunciated it for him. 'Gold-ee-locks.'

He gripped the bars of his cot and with manic strength wrenched them out of my hands and brought the side crashing down. There was nothing between us, I was nose to nose with his fury.

'Listen,' I said, 'if you don't like that story.' He must have got his yellow eyes from his father, the mine-sweeper, because Nell's are blue. Diggory's have a dangerous glint. He started pulling himself upright by the bars of his cot. 'Wait,' I said.

The Voice has always been still and small, it starts in the cage under my ribs, I don't make prior demands about what I want to hear, I take what comes. And the words came. 'Tiger, tiger, burning bright, in the forests of the night' – the words of the book I'm going to write – for children. It will be a classic, but not like *Alice* or *What Katy Did*. It will be about life in the round, about getting ahead, getting ideas, getting hurt. There'll be something about losing, but more about winning.

'Long, long ago, Tiger ruled the forest. He was strong and fierce and ate people. But he was no match for Spider who could take human shape, be a bald fat man or a red-haired woman. Or both at once.

'Tiger was jealous of Spider's gifts. He made up his mind he would eat Spider. Twice over. But first he had to catch him.'

Diggory was all attention, every rabbit on his sleeping-suit stilled. Teachers shouldn't try to be understood. Not understanding is a condition of life in the round, and they should prepare children for it.

'Now Spider was vain about his legs. They were black and slender, he had sixteen and ran on all of them at once. It made him faster than Tiger, the fastest in the forest, he could run rings round the lightning.

'Tiger had the best teeth in the business, but not much else in his head. He went to a wise woman and asked how he could catch Spider. She said, get him to a honey-hole, his legs will stick in the honey and you'll be able to eat him. Tiger said he didn't want Spider's legs, he wanted the bald man for breakfast and the red-haired lady for lunch.'

Diggory chuckled. I had to smile at the Voice's sense of humour.

'The wise woman said it was the easiest thing. Tiger must wait for Spider to change into human form, then he would have only two legs to run with and could easily be caught. She made Tiger fetch her a chicken for troubling her with a silly question.

'Tiger waited and waited and Spider ran about on his sixteen legs but didn't change shape. Tiger had a brilliant idea, at least he thought it was brilliant. He told Spider he knew of a honey-hole in the stump of a tree with more honey in it than anyone could eat. What of it, said Spider, I don't like honey. Ladies do, said Tiger. Give her a treat.

'Spider said, show him the hole and he'd think about it. Tiger took him to the tree-stump and Spider asked him to turn his back while he changed. When Tiger looked round, the red-haired girl was at the honey-hole. Tiger sprang, the girl ducked. He landed on the honey-hole. A swarm of bees came out and stung him unmercifully. Tiger ran, but he wasn't fast enough. The bees went with him. The girl helped herself to honey and went back to her web.'

The Voice ceased.

'A Nancy!' cried Diggory, standing tall in his cot.